THE YOUNGEST GOALIE

Albert Forrest and his teammates with Colonel Boyle
outside of Dey's Arena in Ottawa.

THE YOUNGEST GOALIE

The adventures of a hockey legend

Brian McFarlane

Deneau Publishers
760 Bathurst Street
Toronto, Ontario
M5S 2R6

Cover art: John Booth

Copyright 1989

Printed and bound in Canada

Canadian Cataloguing in Publication Data
McFarlane, Brian, 1931-
  The youngest goalie

ISBN 0-88879-185-2

I. Title.

PS8575.F37Y6 1989   jC813'.54   C89-095076-8
PZ7.M33Yo   1989

Contents

Preface

This is the story of seventeen-year-old Albert Forrest, a remarkable young man who was the central figure in the most incredible challenge for the Stanley Cup. It is the story of the youngest goalie ever to compete for hockey's most famous trophy. It is a story based on truth.

Shortly after the turn of the century, in December, 1904, Albert and his teammates on the Dawson City Nuggets embarked on a 4,000 mile journey to Ottawa, where they clashed with one of the greatest teams ever assembled, the Ottawa Silver Seven. Incredibly, some of the boys from the Yukon started out for Ottawa on their bicycles.

A natural athlete, Albert was a champion cyclist, ball player and speed skater. He was persuaded to become a goalie on short notice during hockey's primitive days, when players were amateurs and any team with a respectable record could challenge for the Stanley Cup.

But the story of Albert Forrest's epic journey to Ottawa and back is more than a hockey story. It sheds a glimmer of light on life in Canada almost a hundred years ago.

Young Forrest was involved in many exciting events as a teenager, including the Klondike gold rush, but his greatest adventure was his quest for hockey's most prized trophy. And while the name Forrest is nowhere to be found among the hundreds of famous hockey names engraved on the surface of the

Stanley Cup, the fascinating story of his gallant bid to place it there deserves to be told.

Perhaps someday there will be a special niche for Albert Forrest in the Hockey Hall of Fame. For he rightfully deserves to be regarded as a genuine hockey legend.

Brian McFarlane

Acknowledgments

The author is indebted to those who encouraged me and assisted me in this project, including Mr. Paul Bergeron of Montreal, Constance Valois of La Tuque, Quebec, Philip Forrest of Everett, Washington, John Columbo, Jack McClelland, Denis Deneau and editor Cindy Dymond of Toronto and Ted Harrison of Whitehorse, the Yukon's most famous artist.

Authors always appreciate the support and input of family members. My thanks to wife Joan, son Michael and daughters Lauren and Brenda, and my sister, Norah Perez, of Youngstown, New York.

My late father, Leslie McFarlane, who gained fame but little fortune as the original author of the Hardy Boys books under the name Franklin W. Dixon, and who wrote the most exciting hockey fiction I ever read, provided the inspiration. This book is dedicated to his memory.

ALBERT FORREST'S JOURNEY TO THE 1905 STANLEY CUP

WALKING
STEAMSHIP
TRAIN

1

Off to the Gold Fields

"Here she comes!"

Albert Forrest watched in awe as the Canadian Pacific transcontinental train, spewing smoke and steam, pulled into the small railway depot in Three Rivers, Quebec. Eleven-year-old Albert and his brothers Paul, nine, and Emil, seven, covered their ears when a sudden shriek of the train whistle warned the people gathered on the platform to stand well back from the gleaming tracks. Albert's brothers didn't need a warning. One look at the huge engine rumbling toward them and Paul and Emil bolted. They dove behind a pile of trunks and suitcases, where they hoped to be safe from the hissing metal monster.

Smiling, Albert took his brothers by the hand, hauled them from their hiding place and convinced them that the mighty engine had no intention of "blowing them to smithereens," as Paul had feared. Nor was it likely to leap off the tracks and swallow them up, a possibility that had occurred to Emil.

The boys' fear of the locomotive and its piercing whistle was not surprising. In 1898, the year our story begins, trains were a novelty in most Canadian towns and villages. Certainly none had ever been seen in Mount Carmel, the small village near Three Rivers where the Forrest family lived. Of the Forrest boys, only Albert, on a trip into town with his father several weeks earlier, had seen a train up close. At the time, he'd been frightened of the noise and the hissing steam too. Now, in just a few moments, he and his brothers were about to experience the thrill of riding in one of these marvelous machines.

Albert led Paul and Emil to a spot on the station platform where their parents were being embraced by a group of neighbors and relatives. Everybody seemed to be shouting "Goodbye" and "Good Luck" and "We'll miss you" to Mr. and Mrs. Forrest. Then the boys were scooped up and subjected to many hugs and kisses from cousins, aunts and uncles. Little Evelyne, age five, the youngest of the Forrest children, was there too, held firmly in the arms of Aunt Estelle. It had been decided that Evelyne was too young to embark on the long family journey. She would stay behind and live with her aunt while the rest of the Forrests were away. Mrs. Forrest could hardly bear to give up her only daughter and was persuaded to do so only when Mr. Forrest vowed they would send for Evelyne soon.

Albert whispered in his sister's ear. "We'll miss you, Ev, and we'll see you again soon. Remember we all love you."

Then, with a jovial conductor offering them a helping hand, the Forrests boarded the train. Mr. Forrest stepped nimbly aboard, then turned on the top step for a final word to the people below. "Thanks for coming," he shouted. "And now we're off. Off to the gold fields. Our great adventure is underway."

When the Forrests were seated on the train, Albert looked out the window. Friends were still waving from the platform. But the tear-stained face of Evelyne brought a lump to his throat. His sister waved a small mittened hand in his direction. Then she turned away, tucking her curly head deep into her aunt's broad shoulder.

"We'll send for you, Evelyne," Albert wanted to shout. "Honest we will. Dad promised." But he knew she would never hear him through the thick glass window.

Then the train gave a lurch and their long journey began.

As the train gained speed, leaving Three Rivers far behind, Albert felt like pinching himself. He could hardly believe all the things that had happened in the past few days. Just a week ago, he had been playing hockey with his brothers and some friends on the frozen creek behind the Forrest house when his father had called across the backyard.

"Albert, bring the boys. Come quick! I have something to tell you."

"But Dad, the score's tied and . . ."

"No buts. You can finish the game tomorrow. This is more important than a backyard hockey game."

Reluctantly, and yet curious to know what their father had to say to them, the boys slipped off their skates on the back steps, threw jackets, scarves and mitts aside and stepped into the kitchen.

At the kitchen table, their father put down his newspaper and peered at them over his spectacles.

"Sit down, boys. Your mother and I have something to say to you. Something important."

At the stove, Mrs. Forrest turned away from the pot she was stirring and smiled at her sons. When she saw the what-have-we-done-now? look on their faces, she added, "Don't worry. Your father has some good news for you, some really exciting news."

"Have you boys ever heard the word Klondike?" Mr. Forrest asked.

Albert glanced at his younger brothers. When they shrugged and looked blank, he answered, "No, Dad, what's a Klondike?"

Mr. Forrest smiled. "The Klondike is a place, Albert, not a thing. It's quite a marvelous place many hundreds of miles from here. It's away up in northern Canada, up in the Yukon territory."

He tapped the newspaper with his finger.

"All the papers lately have had stories about the Yukon and the Klondike gold fields. Smack dab in the middle of the Yukon there's a boom town called Dawson City. It's a place where gold was discovered recently, incredible amounts of gold. Gold nuggets are popping out of the ground like mushrooms. There's tons of gold. All folks have to do is go up there and scoop it up. It's the opportunity of a lifetime for us."

"Does that mean you're going there, Dad?" Albert asked.

3

"No, it means we're all going there," said Mr. Forrest, his bright eyes gleaming behind the spectacles. "It means we're going to leave this place just as fast as we can. I'll sell the house or rent it. Then we'll travel by train all the way from Three Rivers to Vancouver, which is away at the other end of Canada."

He took a salt shaker and swept it across the pine tabletop which served as a map of the nation. "Then we're going this way, north by steamship to a seaport in Alaska." The salt shaker changed course, almost upsetting the sugar bowl, and speedily reached a new destination. "After that, we'll climb some mountains and sail down a big river" (the salt shaker leaped in the air briefly and skidded along the table) "and we won't stop until we reach Dawson City. It's the fastest-growing city in the world, boys. That's where we're going and that's where we're going to get rich."

He tapped the shaker on the table two or three times, then released it. "Boys, you are about to begin the biggest adventure of your lives. You'll see more sights and have more fun than you ever believed possible. And when we claim our share of all that gold, I'll buy you anything you want. Well, almost anything."

"I'd really like a new hockey stick," said Emil. "A good one, like Albert's."

"I'll buy you a dozen sticks, Emil," chuckled Mr. Forrest, reaching over to ruffle Emil's hair. "I'll buy you a hundred sticks. And new skates for all of you. In the Yukon, there's so much ice you can play hockey every day for months."

Albert's mind was a whirl. The idea of moving to a far off place like the Yukon came as quite a shock. He'd miss his friends at school. He'd won a part in the Christmas play, he was a forward on the school hockey team and he was looking forward to playing baseball in the spring. But the thought of finding gold nuggets as big as mushrooms and becoming rich was very exciting. Dawson City sounded like a fascinating place, all right. Especially if there was ice for hockey most of the year.

Albert thought of other exciting things. He'd never been on a train or a ship. In school, his teacher had talked about the marvels of rail travel and how it was now possible to travel by train from one end of Canada to the other. Miss Lapointe had said that trains went right through mountains out west, snaking through long tunnels blasted out of hard rock. He found that hard to believe until she showed the class pictures of the tunnels in a book.

Albert's father knew all about trains. A few months earlier, he'd been all the way to California and back by train. That was on another gold-seeking adventure, one that ended in failure. Now the rest of the Forrest family would discover what it was like to hurtle over the rails at breakneck speed. They would travel to a land of ice and snow where golden nuggets lay gleaming all around.

2

A Tragedy at Sea

It didn't take long for Albert to discover that train travel was far less glamorous than his father had described it. Mr. Forrest had booked the cheapest type of accommodation and the coaches were warm and crowded. At night, it was difficult sleeping on the hard upper bunks. After a couple of days the boys were red-eyed, bored and quarrelsome.

Most disappointing to Albert was the weather. Rain and snow made it hard to see out the grimy window and he was unable to enjoy all the sights he'd been told would make the trip west so worthwhile.

Then, somewhere east of Winnipeg, the flu bug invaded the train and dozens of passengers became ill. Albert and his brothers were among the first to be afflicted. They were sick for the rest of the journey and when the train finally pulled into Vancouver, they were happy the long, dismal ride had finally ended.

In 1898, Vancouver was just beginning to develop into one of the world's most beautiful seaports. The railroad, which began bringing passengers to the west a dozen years earlier, guaranteed the city's future as a center of trade and commerce while the placid blue-green harbor lured ships from distant lands. From the window of their small hotel, Albert and his brothers marveled at the towering snow-capped mountains surrounding Vancouver. They enjoyed watching high-booted people moving through the muddy streets below. Men and women elbowed their way into the Hudson's Bay Company store and emerged laden down with supplies of all descriptions: cans of food, small stoves, heavy coats, hats and gloves, bags of flour and sugar.

"I know who they are and what they're doing," Albert exclaimed, nudging his brothers. "They're gold-seekers. They're stocking up for the trip to the gold fields. Sometimes they're called sourdoughs or stampeders. And that's what we're going to be."

"We're going to be sourdoughs?" asked Paul, wrinkling his nose. "What a funny name. What does it mean?"

"It's the name of a heavy bread people make on the trail," Albert said. "And I guess where we're going we'll be eating a lot of it too."

From Vancouver the Forrests booked passage on a rusty old steamship – the *Amur* – sailing for a place called Skagway, a busy seaport far to the north on the coast of Alaska.

The Forrests were amazed when they boarded the *Amur*. The small ship, with space for sixty, managed to cram in a couple of hundred passengers, all hoping to get rich in the gold fields. The Forrests were forced to share their small cabin with another family of four. That meant the children had to sleep in shifts – when they could sleep at all. Most of the time they were seasick and Albert would remember it for the rest of his life as a miserable voyage. He would also remember it as a voyage marred by a human tragedy.

Aboard the *Amur*, there was barely room to move on deck. Passengers were bedded down everywhere. Several dogs howled their displeasure. Horses tethered to a rail near the engine room whinnied nervously whenever the *Amur* crashed into a particularly high wave. Shortly after leaving port, when the old ship entered some rough seas, a blast of the foghorn startled the horses. One or two panicked and snapped their halters. There was a great scramble on the slippery deck to avoid their flailing hooves.

A young man on his honeymoon was knocked flying by one of

the horses. He skidded along the deck and, with a cry, slipped overboard. His bride screamed and tried to save him, and for a few seconds she was able to cling to his sleeve. Then the ship heaved, she lost her balance and toppled over the rail into the turbulent sea.

While strong men grappled with the horses, others rushed to the rail. Albert searched frantically for a life preserver and finding one, thrust it into the hands of a husky crew member. Mouth agape, the sailor stared in astonishment at the flailing couple in the water. He seemed oblivious to the life preserver.

Albert pulled on the sailor's sleeve. "Please, mister, throw it!" he shouted. "Throw it to them!"

The sailor fumbled with the life preserver. He gave Albert an agonized look, then tossed the life preserver awkwardly into the waves. To everyone's dismay, it fell far short of the couple in the water.

Albert groaned in disappointment. The sailor bellowed "Man overboard!" and stumbled toward the bridge, leaving Albert to haul in the life preserver. Suddenly Albert's father, emerging from below decks, was beside him. "Let me do it, lad," he said grimly. He grabbed the yellow ring and threw it high and far into the ship's wake. But by now the ship had moved still farther from the couple in the water. Albert saw a white hand rise from the waves, reach desperately for the life preserver and fail to grasp it. Then the hand was gone.

By the time the grim-faced captain could turn the heavy ship around, the honeymoon couple had disappeared beneath the waves. The captain, after a brief search, pulled out his pocket watch, studied it a moment, then shrugged and turned the *Amur* north again.

Albert couldn't sleep all that night, thinking of the unfortunate young couple whose dreams of wealth and a long life together were shattered in an instant.

He became upset when he thought of the husky crew member's pathetic attempt to hurl the life preserver. That sailor, he concluded, might have saved two lives if he'd kept his wits about him and used his strength to throw the life preserver properly. He should be ashamed to call himself a sailor.

Albert stared at the ceiling of the tiny cabin for a very long time. Just before he dozed off, he prayed that he would grow up to be strong and fit. He prayed for courage in dealing with dangerous situations. And his final prayer was for the young couple whose lives were taken by the unforgiving sea.

3

Skagway and Soapy Smith

When the *Amur* finally steamed into the port of Skagway in Alaska, the passengers became angry and upset. For the captain dropped anchor far out in the bay, refusing to wait for high tide when he would be able to sail the *Amur* closer to the shore.

"I want you off my ship," he bellowed, ordering them into small boats and dumping them out on the muddy beach some distance away. Their possessions followed them, thrown carelessly from a barge into the mud and gravel.

"You better get your things ashore as fast as you can," a sailor warned them. "Tide's movin' in fast. You'll lose everything to the sea if you don't hurry."

The Forrests worked furiously, moving their possessions to a safe place on shore. Seconds after the last box was snatched away, seawater covered the spot where it had stood.

That's when Albert discovered that his most prized possession was missing. The hockey stick he'd slipped between the straps encircling a steamer trunk, the stick he'd insisted on bringing with him, was nowhere to be seen.

"There it is, Albert," Paul shouted, pointing at the rising water. "There's your stick but it's floating away. You'll never get it now."

Albert was about to wade into the water after his stick when he felt a hand on his shoulder. "Let me take care of this, lad," a friendly voice said. A stranger wearing high boots and a broad-brimmed hat strode into the water until it was up to his knees.

Gracefully, he scooped the hockey stick from the sea and returned it to Albert, who thanked him profusely.

"It must have worked loose from the steamer trunk," Albert said. "And I didn't notice. I've carried it with me all the way from Three Rivers."

"Well, it's a good thing we got it back, then," said the stranger. "I'm a hockey fan myself and I know that good sticks are hard to come by, especially in this part of the country. You a pretty good player?"

Albert grinned and replied honestly, "Well, I guess I'm pretty good compared to most boys my age. But I hope to become a whole lot better. Especially if there's lots of ice in Dawson City to play on."

The stranger turned from Albert and introduced himself to Mr. and Mrs. Forrest. "Hi, folks. My name is Jeff Smith but every-body in Skagway calls me Soapy. Looks like you people could use some help. You can store all your belongings in one of my sheds if you like. Won't cost you anything. I practically run things here in Skagway and I'd like to show you and your boys some true northern hospitality. We're good people here, not like the cap-tain of that ship you just left."

Albert was impressed. He'd never seen a man wearing such fine clothes. And he really liked Mr. Smith's broad-brimmed hat. Mr. Smith had a pleasant voice and a nice smile. Albert thought he saw a pearl-handled revolver tucked into Mr. Smith's belt but a well-tailored topcoat covered it, if it was there at all.

Albert was really surprised when his father politely refused Mr. Smith's offer to help. "Thank you, sir," his father said, "but my sons and I can manage this inconvenience quite easily. I've already arranged for storage until we can be on our way to the gold fields."

"Ah, yes, the gold fields," answered Mr. Smith. "Your son tells me you're headed for Dawson City. Then let's hope you'll return to Skagway soon with a poke full of nuggets."

Albert spoke up. "What's a poke, Mr. Smith?"

11

Mr. Smith smiled at Albert. "Why, it's a small leather bag a sourdough uses to keep his gold dust in. Like this one." He pulled a bag from his coat pocket and shook several small nuggets from it. They rolled around in the palm of his hand.

"Wow!" said the three Forrest boys in unison.

"So that's what real gold looks like," said Emil.

"If you're going to seek it, you'll need some good maps and some advice about campsites in the Yukon," said Mr. Smith. "You better come over to my saloon in town and I'll make sure you're outfitted properly."

Then he reached into another pocket and turned to the boys.

"Say, I just happen to have some sweets here. And some apples in this bag. You boys look mighty hungry so you can share these. Your folks must be very proud of such handsome young men."

He tipped his hat toward Mrs. Forrest. "You've a fine family, ma'am. Welcome to Skagway. If I can be of service to you, remember the name Soapy Smith. It's a name to be trusted. Ask anybody in Skagway."

He shook Mr. Forrest by the hand and moved off down the beach.

Albert watched him for a moment, then turned to his father. "Are we going, Dad? Are we going to Mr. Smith's saloon? Why, he's the nicest man we've met on this trip."

"And the best-dressed," added Paul.

"I'll bet he'll have more sweets for us, too," was Emil's only comment.

Mr. Forrest said, "No, boys, I don't think we'll be visiting Soapy Smith in his saloon. I have a strange feeling about Mr. Smith. I've met smooth talkers like him in California. You have to be very careful who you do business with when there's gold around. There's something about Soapy Smith that bothers me. Maybe it's his name. Soap is slippery, you know. I think we'll buy our maps and supplies someplace else."

Surprised by his father's suspicions, Albert stared once again at the retreating figure of Soapy Smith. Perhaps there's a side to Mr. Smith I didn't notice, he thought.

Albert's brothers were disappointed. "I think Daddy's mean not to give Mr. Smith our business," said Paul, "especially after he saved your hockey stick, Albert, and gave us these apples." From the paper bag Mr. Smith had tossed to him, Paul handed each of his brothers an apple. Hoping they wouldn't notice, he pocketed the biggest one for himself.

Within hours, Mr. Forrest had found a storage shed for their belongings, located a campsite on the edge of town, pitched their sturdy tent and fired up the stove. Then he walked into Skagway to buy maps and supplies.

He was back sooner than anyone expected and he had a man with him. The man's clothes were torn, one eye was swollen shut and Mr. Forrest supported him with one arm. A large husky dog followed on the stranger's heels.

"Found this poor fellow lying in a snowbank," Mr. Forrest explained. "Albert, throw a blanket around him and fix him some tea while I get a chunk of ice to put on his eye. Paul, see if you can find some scraps of food for his dog."

In a few minutes the man was able to sit up and sip the hot tea. He thanked them all for taking him in. Then he told them his sad story.

"I was down at Soapy Smith's buying supplies for my trip to Dawson," he said. "Had five hundred dollars with me and Soapy introduced me to some fellows who said, 'How about a friendly card game?' In minutes all my money was gone. I should have knowed it was a crooked game. But what could I do? When I accused the dealer of cheating, he pulled a gun on me and threatened to shoot me. Then those fellers dragged me outside and beat me up."

"Was Soapy there? Do you think he had something to do with this?" asked Mr. Forrest.

The man shook his head. "No, I don't think so. Soapy left before the trouble started. Soapy seems like a good feller with a big heart. Heck, I'm not the first sourdough to run into trouble like this. And with others who've been swindled, Soapy's been known to give them money for their passage home. Right out of his own pocket."

"What are you going to do now, mister?" Albert asked.

"Go home, I guess. Got a wife and baby back in California. First I'll see Soapy. Maybe he'll help me out. Say, you folks want to buy my dog? His name is Brandy and he's the best dern dog you'll ever see. I can use the money to buy me some new clothes and bunk in somewhere until the next ship comes in." A deal was quickly arranged and Brandy soon found himself inside the tent making friends with the Forrests.

Meanwhile, the stranger left to go back into town where he planned to talk with Soapy Smith. He promised to join the Forrests for dinner later that night.

He was smiling when he came back to share their food. "Well, things are looking up," he said. "Look, I bought me some new clothes and I had a good meeting with Soapy Smith. Soapy was really upset when I told him about the beating I got. He said he regretted the incident took place in his saloon. To help make it up to me he gave me money for a steamship ticket home. Soapy's a good man, a generous man. Just like my friends the Forrests."

After dinner, the man hugged Brandy to his chest for a few moments, then shook hands all around and said goodbye. There was a ship leaving in the morning and he planned to be on it.

4

The Day of the Avalanche

The next day Mr. Forrest bought a second-hand sled and some new harness. When Brandy was hitched to the sled he proved to be a strong and willing worker. The husky was eager to get started and soon the Forrests were on the trail that led to the mountain range to the east.

Despite Brandy's great strength, the provisions that Mr. Forrest had bought were so heavy that all the family members had to pitch in to help Brandy move the sleigh along, either by pushing or pulling. It was hard work, especially when the trail began to rise at a sharp angle toward a place high on a hill. It was a city of a thousand tents, a place someone had named Sheep Camp.

Far behind them now was Skagway. Ahead of them lay unknown hardships and danger. Few of the stampeders realized they'd be on the trail for weeks before they would walk the streets of Dawson City. In Dawson, they'd been told, people were plucking nuggets as big as baseballs out of the hills. Tales like that stirred the blood and made the stampeders eager to reach that exciting place.

The Chilkoot Pass was the quickest way to get over the mountains into Canadian territory and eventually to the rivers that flowed to the land of gold. The Chilkoot was much steeper and far more dangerous than the White Pass, an alternate route. But the Chilkoot was a faster route. And people were in a hurry. So thousands of men, women and children took their chances on

15

the Chilkoot, even though the climb up the mountain terrified many of them.

Thousands more, tired, cold and hungry, and fearful of the avalanches that threatened to thunder down on them, turned back, giving up their dreams of finding a fortune in those far-off fields of gold.

It snowed every day at Sheep Camp. Later, Albert was told that seventy feet of snow fell on the mountains during that harsh winter of 1898.

By order of the Canadian North West Mounted Police, all the stampeders had to carry with them enough provisions to last a year in the Klondike. This included hundreds of pounds of food. Only strong, determined men and women could lug that much weight all the way to Dawson. Needless to say, pack horses and dogs were invaluable and the Forrests blessed the day they found Brandy.

In their tent at Sheep Camp, Mrs. Forrest and her sons huddled around the small stove. The boys were cold and pulled their blankets tight around them. Early in the morning, Mr. Forrest and Brandy, each carrying a heavy pack on his back, fell in behind a long line of stampeders. All of them were intent on getting their supplies to the summit and all climbed in single file up the icy mountain trail.

Albert had volunteered to go but his father had said, "No, son. It's too dangerous. Brandy and I will leave our packs at the summit. Then we'll come back for more. It will take several days to finish the job. But coming back down the mountain each time will be fun. The men simply tuck their coattails under them and slide down. It takes hours to get up there, only a few seconds to get back down."

There was one day at Sheep Camp Albert would never forget. It was the day the ground began to shake and he heard people shouting. He pulled open the tent flap and looked out. He was shocked to discover the world outside was a blur of white. Several men, running frantically to keep ahead of a towering, rolling mountain of snow, screamed, "Avalanche! Run for your lives!" Horrified, Albert watched as the awesome white wave swept two men off their feet and swallowed them up. Dozens of climbers caught on the narrow mountain trail were bowled over and sent tumbling down the steep slope where they were buried alive under the river of snow. There was no way of knowing whether Mr. Forrest and Brandy were among them.

Albert's mother, looking over his shoulder, saw that a quick escape was impossible. The wall of snow was moving too fast. She closed the tent flap and clutched her children to her. Then she prayed. She prayed for her husband somewhere high on the trail and she prayed for the survival of her boys. Then, as she braced herself for the stunning blow that would flatten their tent and bury everyone in it, the rumbling noise ceased. Albert cocked his head, listened a moment, then scrambled to his feet. He opened the flap and shouted, "Mom, we're safe! The avalanche didn't quite reach us." There were tears in his eyes when he turned and said, "But I don't see Dad or Brandy anywhere."

Albert could hear the muffled screams of those trapped under the crush of the avalanche. He saw wild-eyed men don snowshoes and scramble about on rescue missions, shouting directions at each other. People half-buried under the snow wailed for help while men and women floundered through the drifts calling out for loved ones. Albert's brothers were sobbing. They knew something tragic had happened and they feared their father was never coming back. Mrs. Forrest threw on a scarf and gloves, grabbed a small shovel and slipped through the tent opening. She left without a word, frightened speechless for the safety of her husband.

In minutes that seemed like hours, she was back. Three young faces brightened when they saw her supporting their father, who stumbled along beside her. Brandy was there too. The boys jumped up and helped their father through the tent opening. He fell heavily on a blanket, gasping for breath.

"The slide almost buried me," he stammered. "But I grabbed Brandy and used my coattails to slide down ahead of it. Part of the avalanche caught up to us and bowled us over. Knocked the wind out of me and scared the heck out of Brandy." He looked up at his family and grinned. "Thank God you're all safe."

Then he stood up. "Hand me that shovel, Albert! I've got to help the others. There are men buried everywhere." And he was gone again.

Albert pulled his toque down over his ears. He slipped his hands into heavy mitts and went outside. All about him, men were shouting and poking holes in the snow with long poles. They were looking for bodies trapped underneath. He saw a group of men, Albert's father among them, shoveling frantically in one place. Then they bent over and hauled a limp body out of the snow. There was a hasty examination and a cheer. "He's alive! He's alive! Get him into a tent!" Then they rushed off and began digging in another spot.

Once again, Albert learned how unpredictable, and how fragile, life can be. He would never forget the stillness and the gloom that settled over Sheep Camp when the frantic search for survivors finally ended late that night. A hundred flares cast dancing light on the snow as the searchers straggled in, many with tears frozen to their cheeks. Sixty people lost their lives that fateful day. But dozens more were saved, thanks to tireless workers like Albert's father, who was the last to put down his shovel.

Albert played his own unique role in the rescue, a role that earned him much praise and a special reward. When the avalanche first threatened to engulf them, Albert was terribly frightened. Later, he was shocked and saddened to learn that two boys he'd been playing with that very morning, twin sons of a dentist from Chicago, were among the victims. Tears stung his eyes when he realized he'd never see their happy faces again.

Albert was very tired, for the events of the past few hours had left him emotionally drained. But an inner voice told him to stay awake, to keep looking for survivors, even though the other searchers were giving up.

Albert didn't have a long pole to poke into the snow like the other searchers. But he had something almost as good, his hockey stick. With Brandy at his heels, Albert crawled up an embankment. He was determined to take a final look at the disaster area. That's when he noticed a tiny piece of cloth half-buried in the snow. It appeared to be one end of a brightly-colored child's scarf.

He crawled toward the scarf. He pulled at it, trying to shake it loose from the chunks of snow surrounding it. Then he heard a faint moan somewhere beneath him. Somebody was trapped below! But where? Albert began to claw at the snow. He used the blade of his hockey stick to push large chunks aside. Brandy, thinking Albert was playing a game, sent more snow flying with his paws. Albert called for help but nobody heard his cries. He dug deeper. He threw hit mitts aside. It was easier to dig bare-handed. Suddenly, he felt something under his numbed fingers. A piece of cloth, the sleeve of a jacket. And he heard a faint cry.

Snow flew from his hands as he exposed a child's dark head and a white face. It was a young girl and she was still alive. She was wedged against a large chunk of snow. Luckily, it had created a small air pocket around her upper body, allowing her to breathe.

The girl's eyelids fluttered and he found himself staring into her pale blue eyes. "Don't worry," he said soothingly, "I'll get you out." She nodded, then slumped back in a faint. Albert redoubled his efforts and soon he had cleared the snow from around her upper body. Then he heard someone call his name.

"Albert! Al-berrt!" It was his brother Paul, looking for him.

"Over here, Paul. Come quickly! You've got to help me."

Soon Paul was at Albert's side. "Oh, Albert," he said, his eyes growing wide, "you've found a body."

"She's not dead," grunted Albert. "Just unconscious, I think. Now grab that leg and pull on it when I tell you." Paul did as he was ordered. "Now pull hard!" Albert commanded. The boys pulled together. In moments, the girl popped free of the snow into the arms of her rescuers.

"We'll have to carry her," Albert said, scrambling to his feet. "You take her legs, I've got her shoulders." The boys struggled through the snow toward the nearest tent.

Before they reached their destination, a sombre group of people loomed up in front of them. The men had long faces and the women were weeping.

"My God, it's unbelievable! It's her!" A tall man with a full beard rushed toward Albert and Paul. He lifted the young girl into his strong arms and looked anxiously into her face. "Is she . . . is she . . ."

"No, sir," Albert said quickly. "She's very much alive. She's just very tired and I believe she's fainted."

"Thank God she survived," the man said, as the boys fidgeted. He looked down at them. "And thank God you found her. You've saved her life. It's truly a miracle."

"It was my brother Albert who found her," Paul piped up. "Dug her out all by himself. Well, I helped a little. And Brandy did too."

"Stay here please, until I come back," the man directed. He rushed toward a tent and soon Albert and Paul could hear cries of rejoicing from within.

"That must be her family," said Paul. "Thanks to you, Albert, they have their daughter back."

"I just hope she'll be all right," murmured Albert. "Doesn't it make you feel good, Paul, to hear how happy they are?" They looked at each other and grinned while Brandy wagged his thick tail.

In a few moments the tall man reappeared and approached the boys. He said, "My wife is a nurse and she feels confident our daughter will be fine in a day or two. But how can we ever reward you for saving her life? You are genuine heroes, both of you, and we'll be eternally grateful to you."

"Albert did all the digging," said Paul. "He's the hero, sir."

Albert gave Paul a look that said hush.

"You are both heroes," insisted the tall man. "If I had any money at all to spare I would reward you with it. But we are desperate and must turn back to Vancouver and give up the chase for gold." He pressed a small jackknife into Paul's hand, saying, "Take this, lad. It belonged to my father." Then he turned to Albert. "I want you to have this lucky talisman, young man. I hope it will bring you good fortune and safe passage wherever you go. Perhaps someday, we'll meet again and I'll be able to reward you more fittingly." The man handed Albert a smooth stone, blue-green in color with strange marks carved on it. So that's what a talisman is, thought Albert.

The man turned to go. Then he said to Albert, "If you ever meet someone with a similar talisman, young man, consider it to be a stroke of great luck. That person and you will be friends for life. However, you may never meet such a person because there are very few talismans like the one you now possess. They are very rare. Now I must go and console my sister. I regret to say her husband was on the mountain when the avalanche struck and . . ." The man paused to brush a tear from his cheek. "And we have abandoned all hope of finding him."

5

Downriver to Dawson

While it was the most difficult challenge they ever faced, somehow the Forrests made it up and over the frightening Chilkoot Pass. Before they started up the mountain, Mr. Forrest tied the members of his family together with a long rope in case one of them slipped and fell off the icy trail. Paul stumbled once, and might have fallen but Brandy, coming up behind, grabbed the rope in his strong jaws, pulled hard and saved Paul from a nasty tumble.

After hours of steady climbing, they finally reached the summit. There they collapsed in the snow, catching their breath.

It was a joy to slide down the far side of the mountain on their sleigh. But again, it was left to Mr. Forrest to retrieve the supplies he'd carefully stashed at the top of the Chilkoot Pass. Several days passed before they were able to move on.

One day, the Forrests arrived at the edge of a frozen lake, Lake Bennett. There they pitched their tent and made a campsite. There were hundreds of people camped by the lake, all waiting for the spring thaw when the ice would break up. Then the mad rush to the gold fields over inland waters would begin anew.

Everyone was busy building a boat. Dozens of boats of all shapes and sizes were under construction. Albert's father joined some men in a tree-cutting expedition. The logs were whipsawed into long boards and the boards were used in the construction of a boat for the Forrests.

In a few weeks, Albert's father finished an odd-looking craft which he christened *Evelyne*. It was eighteen feet long and four feet wide. It had two pairs of oars and a mast which could be rigged with a sail made from a tent-fly. Mr. Forrest applied pitch to the bottom of the boat so that it would not leak. One of the Mounties patroling the country advised, "Build her strong, Mr. Forrest. You've still got hundreds of miles to go, some of it over water that's mean and nasty. When you hit the rapids near Whitehorse the river's going to bounce you around like a bucking bronco."

In the spring, with the ice floes still floating in the lake, the Forrests joined a flotilla of other boats and sailed off toward Dawson. They crossed Lake Bennett and soon found themselves entering the headwaters of the Yukon River.

It was an uneventful voyage until the river narrowed just west of a town named Whitehorse. That's when they faced the foaming waters of Miles Canyon, with the Whitehorse Rapids just beyond.

They held a conference on shore. Mr. Forrest had learned of a safe way around the rapids. For a lot of money, some men would help him haul his boat up the steep cliff beside the gorge. For more money, they'd push his boat on rollers alongside the river. And they'd put *Evelyne* back in the water beyond the rapids. It would take four days to complete the portage and it would eat up most of their remaining funds. The alternative was to boldly challenge the furious waters of the canyon.

"That only takes four minutes," said Mr. Forrest. "But it's extremely dangerous. We could all be killed if I lose control and *Evelyne* crashes into the walls of the gorge."

Earlier that very day, four boats had challenged the rapids. Two made it safely through but the other two had smashed into the walls of the canyon and six people lost their lives. It brought the number of lives lost since the ice left the river to over thirty.

"Others have made it through," said Mrs. Forrest. "Why can't we?"

"We're not afraid, Dad," said Albert. "You'll guide us through. And we'll help on the oars."

So it was decided. Before shooting the rapids, Mr. Forrest wisely asked for advice from a pair of experienced rivermen.

"The secret is to keep your dern boat in the exact center of the river," he was told. "For in the center of the gorge, the water is forced up. If you get careless and let your boat slide off this crest and slip to either side, you'll be smashed to smithereens."

So they set off, slowly at first, then with breath-taking speed as the current gripped *Evelyne* and whipped them into the gorge and the turbulence ahead.

Mr. Forrest used all of his strength on the big steering paddle while the rest of the family strained on the oars. Working together they managed to keep *Evelyne* in the center of the gorge. They were almost through when Albert screamed, "Boulder ahead!" His warning came just in time for Mr. Forrest to twist his big paddle and steer *Evelyne* past the huge rock. There was a grating sound as the boat's hull scraped the boulder. Then *Evelyne* plunged on and soon the frightening gorge was behind them. The perilous ride was over. "Oh, I'm glad Dad listened to the Mountie and built a strong boat," Albert shouted to his brothers. They all settled back, congratulating themselves and laughing.

Only Emil didn't join in.

"If that's what it feels like to ride a bucking bronco, I don't want to be a cowboy when I grow up," Emil said, standing up to rub his tender backside.

Before the day was over, they successfully navigated several other rapids, which, while dangerous, proved to be much less terrifying than their plunge through Miles Canyon.

They rested in Whitehorse for two days, then boarded *Evelyne* for the final leg of their journey. At Five Finger Rapids, they were forced to choose a route through four great walls of rock emerging from the river. Mr. Forrest wisely chose the right hand channel and once again *Evelyne* escaped the clutches of the dancing waters and the jagged rocks below.

24

Finally, *Evelyne* nosed her way around a rocky bluff and there was Dawson City. The Forrests rushed to the bow of the boat and stared open-mouthed at thousands of tents and log shacks that dotted the landscape. Hundreds of boats nuzzled the shore and people were everywhere, rushing about their business. Albert could hear the slam of a blacksmith's hammer, the rasp of a saw and the shouts of children. A man on shore skinning bark from logs waved as they went gliding by. A dozen women washing clothes in the river chatted as they scrubbed. It was an amazing sight, one that Albert would remember for as long as he lived.

Soon the Forrests were part of the thriving tent city. Their tent was surrounded by thousands of other tents—tents of all shapes and sizes and colors, sturdy tents and soggy tents, leaky tents and falling-down tents.

It was often bitterly cold in the Forrest tent. The small stove threw little heat. As summer approached, flies, bugs and mosquitoes boldly invaded their tiny domain.

"Remember how excited we all were about coming on this trip?" Paul asked one day. His lip quivered as he added, "Well, I don't think it's been a fun trip at all. I wish we'd never left Three Rivers."

Emil said, "I hate it here. We've been here for weeks and I've not seen any gold. And we've never enough to eat."

Albert smiled and said, "It's true the nuggets aren't lying around like people said. But they must be here somewhere. Dad will find some soon and make us rich. I know it hasn't been much fun so far for any of us. But things will get better. Dad's going to start work on a log house for us to live in. There's a new school going up and best of all, I heard some men talking about flooding the school yard for a hockey rink. We'd all feel better if we could get out on the ice and play a little hockey."

6

Life in Dawson City

Life in Dawson City became much more pleasant for the Forrests once their log house was finished and they moved in. A wood stove heated the small building. No longer were the boys kept awake by the flapping of canvas whenever the north wind howled. Nor did they have to worry about mud and water seeping under the floorboards of their tent and soaking their bedrolls.

Paul was impressed with the new outhouse his father had constructed in back of the house. Paul bragged to his new friends that it was the only "two-holer" in their part of town.

Mr. Forrest was away from their log home much of the time. He worked long hours on a gold claim he'd staked a few miles downriver from Dawson City. But he never took much gold from the ground. The best claims were already owned by others, men who'd been in the area when news of the gold discoveries reached the world outside. Of the thousands of stampeders who flocked to the Klondike during the great gold rush, only a few struck it rich.

On New Year's Eve, 1899, the last day of the old century, the Forrests celebrated the beginning of a brand new one with a house-warming. It was a grand party with friends and neighbors – about forty of them – squeezing their way into the small home.

When the fiddlers began to play and the dancers stomped the floor, dishes rattled and floorboards creaked. Albert and his brothers, who were allowed to stay up past midnight so they too

26

could greet the twentieth century, feared the chinking they'd worked so hard to wedge between the logs would work loose and tumble to the floor.

Early in 1900, the new schoolhouse opened in town. For months, the boys had received a limited amount of schooling in one of the tents set aside for this purpose. The new schoolhouse had eight rooms, one for kindergarten, three for public school students and three for high schoolers.

Albert enjoyed school, especially the English and history lessons. One day a noted poet, Robert Service, visited the school and read some of his poems to the students. Albert lingered after class and met the poet. Service encouraged Albert to try his hand at writing and even gave Albert a signed copy of one of his poems, which Albert later hung on the wall over his bed.

Albert missed his sister Evelyne for they had been very close. He wrote her letters regularly even though he knew a month might pass before someone traveled "outside" with a bundle of mail to be posted in Vancouver or Seattle.

He wrote his aunt and told her about life in the Klondike, how newcomers were called "cheechakos" by the natives. Of course, they were also known as sourdoughs or stampeders and they were a colorful lot. He wrote about strange people with fascinating names, like Diamond Tooth Gertie, a dancehall girl who had a real diamond imbedded in her tooth. He wrote of Big Alec McDonald from Nova Scotia who traded a sack of flour for a gold claim thought to be worthless. Later it produced millions. There was Swiftwater Bill Gates who owned the only white shirt in town and was so proud of it he only took it off to have it laundered. Swiftwater was said to have bathed in champagne once, although Albert couldn't imagine why anyone would want to do that.

Another time, to annoy a lady friend who had slighted him, Swiftwater bought up every egg in Dawson for five dollars apiece. The lady friend liked eggs and Swiftwater was determined not to let her have any. One old prospector told Albert that Swiftwater fed the eggs to his dogs.

"Threw 'em from his second floor window, he did," said the prospector. "And them dern dogs was leapin' eight feet in the air tryin' to catch 'em. Never saw a sight like it."

He wrote about another prospector who promised to match a dancehall girl's weight in gold if she would promise to marry him. She quickly agreed and the sourdough took $2,500 in gold dust from his poke and placed it on the weigh scales. They're still living happily together, Albert reported, and that happened months ago.

He told her about the men who first discovered gold on Rabbit Creek: Skookum Jim and Tagish Charley and Lying George Carmack who earned his nickname because he was always claiming to have struck it rich when he hadn't. After eleven years of prospecting, he finally did strike gold and lots of it.

He wrote of the prospecting trips he took with his father and how the mosquitoes almost ate him alive the last time they camped out. "The mosquitoes here are as big as bumblebees," he wrote. "And if you swat one, a million of his relatives come after you seeking your blood."

Albert discovered that time passed quickly in Dawson City if he kept busy. He was always busy. There were chores to do every day and lots of homework after school. Then came the best part of the day, free time for playing.

He and his brothers and their friends played hockey every day, either on a nearby frozen creek or on the schoolyard rink. When summer came they turned to soccer and baseball.

Albert was small for his age but very fast. And he had boundless energy. In baseball, nobody could run the bases faster or hit the ball harder than Albert.

His brother Paul would say, "I don't know how you hit the ball so far, Albert. You're such a skinny thing."

In the gym, he could outbox and outwrestle all but the biggest boys.

And whenever the boys jumped on their bicycles and someone yelled, "Race you to the Frontier Saloon and back," nobody could keep pace with Albert's pumping legs and spinning wheels.

One year, with Dawson City growing so big it became the second largest city in Canada west of Winnipeg, the citizens decided to build a huge sports center complete with gymnasium, indoor hockey rink and curling rink. It was to be called the Dawson City Athletic Club. Albert couldn't wait for it to open. Hoping to hurry things along, on weekends he helped the workers by carrying pieces of lumber and buckets of nails. And he brought them water from the well to quench their thirst. When the center finally opened, Albert was among the first to skate on the ice and to test all the equipment in the gymnasium.

By the time Albert was in his teens, he could run like a rabbit, swim like a seal and jump like a grasshopper. He was always bursting into the house, the last boy home from some game or another, late for supper. His mother would say, "Slow down, Albert. You're always running in here puffing like a racehorse." His father would blow on his soup and say, "You're going to run yourself right into the ground, son. No wonder you're small. Save some energy to grow on."

Albert would just grin and reply, "Someday, Mom and Dad, I'm going to be the best athlete in Dawson City. You said it yourself, Dad. If you want to be the best at something, you've got to work at it."

In 1903, the year that Albert turned sixteen, the Dawson City Athletic Club held its first Annual Winter Carnival. People came from miles around, arriving on foot, on snowshoes, by dog sled and by horse-drawn cutter.

Albert and his family tramped through the snow to the arena. Albert and his brothers urged their parents, "Hurry, hurry, please. We want to see all the skating races and we're going to enter as many as we can."

Paul and Emil looked forward to the fun involved in the spoon and egg race, the barrel-jumping contests and the obstacle course in which the contestants had to jump over some obstacles and slide under others. Albert was eager to take part in the sprints, and if the organizers would let him, he'd enter the mile race, the feature event of the evening.

At 5' 4" tall and 140 pounds, Albert never expected to win any of the skating races. He had a reputation for speed, especially on the hockey rink, but he was aware that bigger, stronger, older boys would be competing in all the carnival events. Albert merely wanted to perform well in front of his parents. He hoped to make them proud of him.

But when the bell clanged to start each race, Albert flew away from the pack. He won three sprints easily, surprising himself, flashing over the finish line ahead of competitors four and five years his senior. He even won the barrel-jumping competition and teamed up with Paul to capture the three-legged race.

Everyone cheered Albert. A group of young girls, attracted by Albert's dark good looks, shouted "Go, Albert! Go!" as he sped around the arena in the sprints. But some of the older boys he passed were embarrassed and angry.

"We'll whip you in the distance race, Forrest," one of them told Albert. The speaker, a nineteen-year old named Oscar, a huge lad with bulging muscles, scowled at his young opponent.

"Better steer clear of those fellows in the big race," warned Paul. "They don't like you showing them up."

"I can't very well avoid them," replied Albert. "But I'm not going to let them frighten me off."

When the competitors were called to the starting line for the mile race, Albert was the youngest and the smallest skater in the event. A dozen other boys jostled their way into the best starting positions and Albert found himself shunted aside. He had to start well behind all the others.

But when the race began he moved up quickly. He darted around and between the bigger boys. Some of them tried to block him off. Oscar, the boy with the bulging muscles, elbowed him in the stomach. Albert doubled over for a second or two. Then he caught his breath and got right back in the race.

Albert zigged and zagged until the other racers didn't know

where he was or what he was going to do next. If he spied an opening he'd dash through. When Oscar and one of his burly pals tried to close a gap and sandwich Albert, they bumped heads and fell to the ice. Albert couldn't help smiling when he heard the bullies yelping in his wake.

The spectators, noting Albert's strategy, howled their approval. Another group of girls took up the chant, "Go, Albert. Go, Albert." And when Albert flashed to victory in record time everyone leaped from their seats and gave him a standing ovation. It was the biggest thrill of young Albert's life.

"That was more fun than Christmas," Albert confided to his brothers when they got back home. The boys were sharing a box of apples Albert had won as his prize for winning the big race. Apples were a rarity in the Yukon, especially in winter.

Paul, his cheeks bulging with chunks of the imported fruit, nodded in agreement.

"You were great tonight, Albert. I can't believe you skated so fast."

In the next day's *Klondike Nugget*, the paper's only reporter wrote:

> By winning the mile race in sensational fashion, young Albert Forrest establishes his right to be called the champion skater of the Yukon. He deserves to be recognized as the best skater in the country after his performance in the feature event of last night's Winter Carnival. Unfortunately, Albert will probably never get an opportunity to test his exceptional speed against the best skaters elsewhere, especially in the East. But if he does, this writer feels confident he will show his heels to all of them.

7

A Surprise Invitation to Play

The next day, when Albert, his brothers and his parents were busy nibbling on apples and reading all about Albert's winning performances in the *Klondike Nugget*, a man came to their house.

It was Weldy Young. Everybody in Dawson knew the famous sportsman. Several years earlier, he had been a star player with the Stanley Cup champion Ottawa Silver Seven, the best hockey team in the world. Then, after a dispute with the Ottawa management, he quit the team and took a job with the Canadian government. A few months later he was transferred to the Yukon.

In Dawson City, Young also served as playing-coach of the Dawson City Nuggets, the leading team in the city's popular senior hockey league. Even though he soon would be forty years old, Young still retained the look of a champion and he had no difficulty winning the league goal-scoring championship year after year.

Young's keen eye seldom missed the mistakes of others. As a coach, he was quick to correct those mistakes and the teams he guided always had winning records.

Recently, rumors had spread through Dawson that Weldy Young and a millionaire sportsman named Colonel Joe Boyle were going to organize an all-star hockey team in Dawson, one good enough to challenge the powerful Ottawa champions for the Stanley Cup.

At the Forrest's kitchen table, munching an apple and waiting for the cup of tea he had been offered, Weldy explained the reason for his surprise visit.

"Folks, you've probably heard that Colonel Boyle and I want to bring the Stanley Cup to Dawson. People hereabouts may scoff and say we don't have a chance against Ottawa, the world champions. But I think we do. The best amateur teams in Canada have the right to challenge for it and I think you'll see a Dawson team on its way to Ottawa before the year is out. Now won't that be something. A bunch of goldminers traveling over 4,000 miles to play a couple of hockey games."

"Sounds like a great adventure, Weldy," Mr. Forrest agreed.

"It'll be a stunning upset if Dawson should win," said Albert. "I'll bet outsiders don't even know we have a brand new arena in Dawson, much less a hockey team." Albert, like most Yukoners, always referred to people who lived beyond the mountains as "outsiders".

"That's right, Albert, most of them don't. But they will. And the Ottawa team will probably accept our challenge because they think it'll mean an easy victory. Also, the novelty of a team traveling thousands of miles to play for the Stanley Cup will appeal to them. The Ottawa fans will be lining up to see us play."

"But what's a hockey trip to Ottawa got to do with us, Mr. Young?" asked Mrs. Forrest. "If you're here looking for financial support for such a trip, I'm not sure we're able to contribute very much . . ."

Weldy Young chuckled. "No, I'm not looking for money, Mrs. Forrest," he said. "I'm here because of what young Albert did last night."

The Forrest family exchanged puzzled looks.

"When Albert won those skating races last night," Weldy continued, "I said to myself, now there's a young man with skill and determination. And he's a natural athlete. Plays baseball, soccer, hockey. A bit small perhaps, and awfully young but I can see the makings of a champion in Albert. Reminds me a bit of myself at that age. Could be he's just the lad I need on the team I take to Ottawa."

Albert's jaw dropped. Clearly, Weldy had lost his senses. Why, Albert didn't think he was nearly good enough at hockey to be on a team that challenged for the Stanley Cup. Albert knew all about the Stanley Cup. Donated by Lord Stanley, Canada's Governor General in 1893, less than a dozen years earlier, it was prized by hockey teams everywhere. Only the best amateur players competed for it and sometimes there were two or three challenges for it in a season. But for Albert to play on a challenging team – impossible!

Albert's father must have had similar thoughts for he said, "Weldy, we are all very proud of Albert. We know he's the best speedskater around. And he loves all sports. But let's face it. Albert's just a pond hockey player. He's never been on a real team. You remember what happened when he tried out for the city league this year. They told him to come back in a year or two when he grew up. He'd get killed playing against those roughnecks in Ottawa."

"Not if I played him where they weren't likely to touch him," said Weldy.

"And where would that be?" snorted Mr. Forrest. "Rinks are small and Albert's not the sort to run and hide from anyone."

"I agree," smiled Weldy. "That's why I think Albert should be the goalie on our team."

Around the table, eyebrows shot up. Everyone gaped at Weldy Young in astonishment.

"But Mr. Young, Albert's never been a goalie," stammered Emil.

"That's right. I've never been a goalie," echoed Albert.

"You really believe Albert could be your goalie?" asked Mr. Forrest.

"It's worth a try," answered Weldy Young. "I'll admit it's a gamble. But we don't have a goalie in Dawson. Not any that aren't old, fat or slow. So I thought of Albert. Here's a young lad who does everything well in sports. A natural. So I'll teach him how to play goal. We've got all summer and fall. He can practice. Emil and Paul can shoot pucks at him out by the shed. If Albert's

willing, all I need is your permission. If you think he's too young
. . ."

"Albert is definitely too young," interrupted Mrs. Forrest in a voice strong enough to wake the cat. "He's still my baby. The very idea, Mr. Young, thinking we'd allow Albert to stand in one of those cages while grown men shoot those hard rubber things at his body. It's a ridiculous idea. And even if you made a goalie out of him, there's no way we'd allow Albert to go to Ottawa with you. No, he's too young, it's too far and it's much too dangerous, especially in winter. It's no trip for a teenager, Mr. Young. You should know that. Now if you'll excuse us, it's getting late and the children have to get to bed . . ."

At the door, Weldy Young turned and said, "Perhaps if you talk it over some more . . ."

"No need for any more talk," replied Mrs. Forrest. "Albert is not going to be a goalie, he's not going to Ottawa and that's all there is to it. Thank you for calling, Mr. Young. Now I'll bid you goodnight."

It's a wonder that Albert was able to do it. Somehow he persuaded his mother to change her mind and let him go off to Ottawa and play for the Stanley Cup.

Obviously, his father had a lot to do with the decision. His father said to his mother, "It's true that Albert could be hurt if he plays in goal. It's also true that he's very young to be going on such a long trip. He'll miss a few weeks of school and we'll all miss him and worry about him. But when will he ever get such a chance again? Probably never. Think of all the things he'll see and do. Think of how proud we'll be if he helps the Nuggets win the Stanley Cup and they bring it home to Dawson."

In the end, Albert's mother gave in and Albert was told he could be part of Dawson City's challenge for the Stanley Cup. He started practicing immediately.

Weldy Young brought him some goal pads. They were lightweight, flimsy pads that offered little protection. But Albert thought they were wonderful. He found some old boards and built a backstop, a barrier to stop flying pucks. He found another wide, flat board to use as a base for shooting pucks. And he placed two posts in the ground six feet apart. They served as goal posts.

Every day, he coaxed his brothers to come out and shoot pucks at him. At first, they put the pucks behind him easily. But soon he became accustomed to wearing the goal pads and wielding the battered goal stick Weldy had given him. He learned to deflect pucks with his stick, keeping them out of the goal. Often he'd put the stick down and attempt to stop shots using only his pads. Before long, his brothers found it more and more difficult to score on him.

Summer and fall passed quickly. In late fall the temperatures dropped below freezing and ice returned to the ponds and streams. Albert got out his skates and continued to practice every day. In early December, the Nuggets held several scrimmages as a team and Albert found the shots his teammates took much faster and harder to stop than his brothers. Especially Weldy Young's.

"Weldy might win the Stanley Cup for us all by himself," Albert told his father one day. "He's the best hockey player I've ever seen. And he holds the team together. Some of the men want to loaf or quit practice early if Weldy's not around. But when he's on the ice he cracks the whip and makes sure we do our best."

Mr. Forrest said, "Son, you can learn a lot about a man's character by being on the same team with him. Some players have talent and skill but they're lazy. They don't like to practice. Others don't react well to pressure. They give up and rely on others to come through in the clutch. You'll have learned a lot more about your teammates by the time you get to Ottawa."

Finally, the day of departure arrived. Actually there were two departure days. The players had a choice of walking to Whitehorse or riding their bicycles there. The walkers left on a Friday and the cyclists rode out two days later. They intended to overtake the walkers before they reached Whitehorse. In Whitehorse, the new White Pass Railway Line, which had finally ended the agonizing overland route in and out of the Klondike, would have a train waiting to whisk them to Skagway. Then, after four days at sea on a steamship bound for Vancouver, the Nuggets would board a Canadian Pacific train which would carry them across the nation to Ottawa.

Only two of his teammates, Norman Watt and Hector Smith, joined Albert in the cycling group. Most of Dawson turned out on Sunday to give the three cyclists a memorable sendoff, much like the one they'd given the walkers.

Albert found an old green ledger at home, one his father had planned to use to keep track of his gold discoveries. It had never been opened and Albert asked for it. "I want to take it with me to Ottawa," he explained. "It's going to be my diary."

In the diary, on page one, he wrote:

Sunday, December 21, 1904. All of Dawson turned out to wish us *bon voyage* when Hector, Norman and I mounted our bicycles. The rest have gone ahead and, with luck, we'll catch up to them in a few days. It's 350 miles to Whitehorse and we're praying it doesn't snow and slow us up. It seems strange to be leaving in 1904 for a hockey series that won't begin until 1905, almost a month from now.

I had a big lump in my throat when my family hugged me and wished me good luck. Tears rolled down my mother's cheeks and my dad's eyes were moist too. So were mine. Dad gave me a few extra dollars to spend in Ottawa. Paul wants me to bring him back some apples and Emil said a souvenir hockey puck from one of the big games would be fine with him.

Weldy Young was supposed to join us but at the last minute the government ordered Weldy to stay on in Dawson until the local elections are over. We must have Weldy. Nobody thinks we can win without him. Weldy says he can still get to Ottawa in time for the series if he leaves right after the elections. But we all know bad weather could hold him up. A missed connection – any delay at all – and our best player will be absent when the series begins next month. As we pedaled out of town, hundreds of people ran along beside us, cheering us and wishing us luck. Paul and Emil held tight to Brandy's collar to prevent the husky from following me. Brandy is such a great dog. But he's happiest when there's a trail to follow and a new adventure lurking around every turn.

Only Oscar tried to spoil our departure. He stepped in front of my bike and shouted, "Forrest, you baby. You're not man enough for such a long trip. When it gets cold and dark tonight along the trail, you'll come running back cryin' for your mommy."

For the first hundreds yards, Oscar and his friends lumbered along beside me, taunting me. But when I made a sudden movement, turning my front wheel toward them, they stumbled into each other and fell over in a heap. Everyone laughed. I turned and waved at the crowd. They all waved back until the three of us entered the woods and were lost from sight. We were on our way.

8

A Dramatic Rescue on the Trail

First it was the wind, howling an eerie warning before sweeping down from the mountains and into the valley, lifting leaves and twigs in its path and hurling them pell mell against rocks and bushes lining the trail.

Then it was the snow. Nothing more than a wind-tossed sprinkle of flakes at first, followed quickly by a furious assault of crystals that blinded the bikers, forcing them to dismount. Heads buried against their chests, mittened hands shading squinted eyes, they struggled on, three weary snowmen with one thought in mind – to reach the Northwest Mounted Police post, still six long miles away.

An hour later, the squall behind them, they were back on their bikes. Tires left graceful trails in their wake. Small drifts of snow in the path ahead were skirted with care. Then, to their dismay, and occurring so suddenly it caught them totally by surprise, there was a serious accident.

Hector, who was leading the way along a steep downhill run, crashed into a pile of small rocks hidden under the snow. The rocks, washed across the trail weeks earlier by a flooded stream, stopped Hector's bike. But they didn't stop Hector. He flew over the handlebars and tumbled down an embankment. Unable to stop, he splashed headlong into the turbulent waters of the Yukon River. Bruised and shocked, Hector screamed for help. But help was slow in coming. Albert and Norman, following close behind when Hector struck the rocks, tried to apply their

39

brakes. Too late. They too skidded into the rocky pile. They were flung from their bikes, and tumbled to the ground.

Norman lay moaning, clutching his knee. Albert was shaken up but ignored his own bumps and bruises. Hector was in trouble, big trouble, and he needed help. Hobbling to the edge of the embankment, Albert looked over. Hector was struggling in the black current. He clung to the branch of a small bush and cried out. "Help me, Albert! Hurry! I can't swim and I can't hold on much longer. My hands are freezing."

Stay calm, Albert told himself. Stay calm and don't panic. Decide quickly what's best to do and then do it. He yelled at Hector, "You can hang on. You must. For just a few seconds." Then Albert leaped up and ran back to Norman, who had struggled to his feet and was limping in small circles.

"Norman, come on. I need your help RIGHT NOW! Drag your bike over to the river bank. Hec's in the water and I'm going in after him. But neither of us will be able to get back up the slope unless you help us. It's too slippery. Slide your bike over the slope and hang on tight to one wheel. We'll grab the other wheel. We're counting on you to haul us out. Now move!"

Norman nodded and limped away to retrieve his bicycle. Albert, praying that Hector hadn't let go of the branch, all that protected him from an icy death, raced back to the embankment and peered over. Hector was still struggling in the water but his fingers were slowly slipping down the branch. Another few seconds and he'd be swept away.

Albert took a quick breath and slipped over the edge. He skidded down the embankment and plunged into the water just as Hector's fingers released the branch. Albert gasped as the frigid water engulfed him but he managed to reach out and grasp Hector firmly by the collar of his heavy jacket. Hector groaned and coughed. They were only a few feet from shore but it took all of Albert's strength and swimming skills to battle the swift current and fight his way back to the river bank. By the time he felt the river bottom under his boots, Hector was almost unconscious.

Don't give up, Albert told himself as he hauled Hector out of the water. All we have to do now is get up that icy embankment. After that we'll worry about finding shelter. He looked up and saw the white face of Norman Smith, hands locked firmly around the crumpled rim of his bicycle wheel. The other wheel dangled just within reach. Albert maneuvered Hector's heavy body into position.

"Hector, hang onto the wheel," Albert barked. "And hang on tight!" Groaning and spitting water, Hector reached up to obey. Then, with Norman pulling from above and Albert pushing from below, the bicycle, with Hector clinging to it, was dragged slowly but steadily up the steep incline. When Hector reached the brink, he had just enough strength left to roll himself over the lip onto flat ground. He lay there gasping for breath, thankful to be alive.

Norman yelled down at Albert. "Hector's up and he's safe. Now it's your turn. Grab the wheel, Albert!"

Albert's teeth were chattering and his fingers were numb. I may not be able to hang onto the wheel, he thought. And there's nobody behind me to push me up.

But then another voice intruded in his thoughts. Of course you'll make it, the other voice said. You're young and strong. And you've got pride haven't you? You're not going to topple back into the river and drown. What would everybody say? That Albert tried hard but when he found himself in a tight spot he gave up? Now, Albert, grab that wheel and get yourself out of this fix.

Albert reached for the dangling wheel of the bicycle, wrapped his numb fingers around the rim in a painful grip and shouted up at Norman, "Haul away!" Norman, wheezing and grunting, pulled from above, using all of his ebbing strength. Albert, clinging with both hands to the bicycle rim, started up the slope. He dug his toes into small footholds and strained to keep from slipping back into the river. The minute or so it took for Albert to climb to safety seemed like ten, perhaps twenty minutes. But he made it. When he rolled over the brink and rose unsteadily to

41

his feet, he turned to Norman and grinned. Norman grinned back and laid a hand on Albert's shoulder. "That was a close call," he said. "Albert, you're quite a hero. You saved Hector's life."

"It's not saved yet, Norman. If we don't find shelter or get a fire going, Hector's not going to make it. He'll freeze to death. And so will I."

"The mounted police post can't be very far down the trail," said Norman. "We could get a fire started here but that takes time and it's getting dark. It's your call, Albert."

Albert looked at Hector, who had struggled to his feet and was moving about. Tiny icicles clung to his mustache. He stamped his feet and coughed. Albert took Hector by the shoulders and peered into his eyes.

"Hector, can you walk? If you can, we'll try for the police station. If you can't, we'll try to light a fire."

"I'll do whatever you want, Albert," mumbled Hector through chattering teeth. "I can't thank you enough for getting me out of that river. I thought I was a dead man for sure."

"Never mind that now, Hector. I think you can walk well enough to reach the outpost. We'll leave the bikes here. They're no more use to us anyway. Now let's go. We've wasted too much time already."

They gathered up their packs and were soon on their way. Albert set the pace. His clothes were frozen to his back. He had no feeling in his fingers. He'd gone just a few paces when Norman took him by the arm, forcing him to turn.

"Here, Albert. Take these." Norman held out his mitts. Albert was about to protest when Norman hushed him. "I know you lost yours in the river. You can have mine." He took Albert's stiff hands and forced the mitts on over them. "Now, lead on, Albert."

Albert was grateful to Norman. He's a man I can count on when trouble arises, Albert thought. And I know he has new-found respect for me. I could see it in his eyes back there by the river.

They had shared a dangerous situation, one that might have ended in disaster. And they had survived. I've learned something from that experience, Albert thought. I've learned not to panic or give up when things look hopeless. Even when you're more frightened than you've ever been in your life.

It was an agonizing walk to the police post. Several times Hector staggered and almost fell. Each time, Norman and Albert hauled him upright and urged him to keep moving. Desperately cold and almost totally exhausted, they were about to drop in their tracks when Albert shouted, "Ho! Lights ahead." Through the trees, he saw the yellow light from a window. It was the mounted police post, a few hundred yards away. He turned, waiting for his mates to catch up, and saw that Hector had fallen again. He was stretched out in the snow.

With strength he didn't know he possessed, strength born of a desperation to reach his goal, Albert hoisted Hector over his shoulder and carried him the rest of the way.

Fortunately, Constable Quinn of the Northwest Mounted Police had been expecting them. There was a pot of stew bubbling on the stove. When the Mountie saw the condition they were in, he threw more wood on the fire and helped them out of their heavy clothes. He examined Hector, looking for signs of frostbite, then turned to his companions. "Not much wrong with your friend that a good night's sleep and some warm food won't cure."

He noticed Albert wringing water out of a pant leg.

"Had a little swim, did you, son?" he quipped. "Well, it's late in the season for water sports but I suppose you athletes like to stay active."

He didn't expect an explanation. Not then. That would come later, when teeth stopped chattering and bodies stopped shivering.

"Gather round the stove, boys, and dry yourselves out," he ordered. "Then we'll get you fed and you can tell me what happened. By the way, your teammates were here yesterday. Left early this morning and should be about thirty or forty miles ahead of you. They said you'd be coming by bicycle. I was going to ride into Dawson today but they asked me to wait for you. Now tell me what happened? How'd you get so wet?"

Norman, who was in better condition to talk than the other two, told the story of Hector's near-fatal plunge into the river and how Albert coolly jumped in and rescued him. Constable Quinn looked at Albert appraisingly and said, "Well, now, that's something, isn't it?" Then, noting that his visitors had almost stopped shivering, he moved to the stove and ladled out large bowls of stew. Moments later, he produced some hard biscuits and cups of steaming tea.

When the men were nearly finished their meal, Constable Quinn wiped his mustache and said casually, "I see you enjoyed my simple cooking, men. I was lucky to trap a couple of rats this morning. Nothing like rat stew to fill an empty stomach."

Albert looked up, his eyes wide. "Rat stew?" he choked, dropping his fork to the floor. Albert loathed rats.

The others looked surprised. "I had to make do," Constable Quinn chuckled. "I wanted to make beef stew but the butcher shop was closed today." He fished a piece of meat out of his bowl and began chewing on it. "Mmm-mm," he said, "Delicious. Now Albert, if you're brave enough to pull drowning people from the river surely you're brave enough to savor my rat stew."

Albert gulped and got up from the table. Suddenly he didn't feel very well. Then, when he noticed the others choking back their laughter, he realized he'd been the butt of a joke. And his teammates had been in on it.

But he made a quick recovery. Sheepishly, he sat down, retrieved his fork, and said with a broad grin. "Constable, do you suppose I could have another bowl of your delicious rat stew?"

"Rat stew, Albert?" laughed the Mountie, passing the pot across the table. "Son, you must have heard me wrong. This is rabbit stew. Didn't you hear me say I snared two of them this morning?"

"Don't mind Albert," chuckled Norman, wiping his eyes. "He

must be going deaf. He's still got some of that river water in his ears."

"What's that, you say?" Albert replied, feigning deafness and cupping his ear. Then Albert appeared to lose control of the stew pot. He yelled, "Look out!" and Norman, thinking the hot stew was going to land in his lap, pushed back from the table and tumbled over backwards to the floor.

Again, the small room rocked with laughter.

"Sorry about that Norman," chuckled Albert as he placed the pot back on the table. He studied his palms. "Looks like I'm losing my grip as well. I guess I still have some of that river water on my hands."

Norman was laughing so hard he couldn't get up.

9

To Whitehorse and Beyond

In the morning, Constable Quinn saddled his horse, waved a cheery goodbye and rode off toward Dawson City. The three hockey players, wearing dry clothes and in good spirits, began walking in the opposite direction, toward Whitehorse, at a brisk pace.

"We'll have to cover over thirty miles a day if we hope to catch the others," said Norman. "And we can't count on running into a good man like Constable Quinn at every outpost. Some posts will be deserted."

The snow began to fall in fat flakes before they reached their next stop, a tumble-down trapper's cabin. There was some canned food in the cabin and a note from their teammates urging them to make good speed. "Try to catch up to us before we reach Whitehorse," the note read. The three men gathered some wood and slept as close as they dared to the glowing fire.

They might never have caught up to their teammates had it not been for the assistance of a pair of Klondikers who overtook them on the trail. The McCarthy brothers, Ben and Bob, were headed for Whitehorse. Each man had a sled pulled by fine-looking dogs.

"Fellers, climb aboard and rest your feet," ordered Ben McCarthy.

"It's your lucky day," added brother Bob. "Our sleds are almost empty. We'll be loading up with supplies in Whitehorse for the return run. But there's plenty of room now."

"And I guarantee we'll make good time," said Ben.

The weary players didn't need a second invitation. Soon they were tucked under blankets on the sleds and flying over the trail behind the yelping huskies. At one stop, the McCarthy brothers brewed hot tea and distributed pieces of cake to the Nuggets. Ben lifted his cup in a salute. "It's Christmas Day, fellers. Maybe you want to think about your families for a moment." When Albert, who had lost track of the date, thought about his family and Christmas Day back in Dawson, he had a lump in his throat the size of a hockey puck.

It took the first group of hockey players nine days to reach Whitehorse. Thanks to the McCarthy brothers, the second group caught up to the first on the outskirts of town where there was a joyful reunion. Players pounded each other on the back and everyone talked at once.

"Where are your bicycles?" asked Sureshot Kennedy. "We expected you fellows to catch up with us a couple of days ago."

Norman told them of the accident with the bicycles, how Hector had landed in the river, and how Albert had bravely jumped in to save his life. He talked of their other adventures and made them laugh when he said, "Why in the world did we set out on this dern trip, anyway? We must all be lunatics."

The McCarthy brothers left to feed their dogs and refused to take any money for helping out. "Just bring back the Stanley Cup, boys," said Ben.

"Yep. That'll be payment enough," added Bob. The two men waved goodbye and drove off.

A few minutes later, with the dark night swiftly surrounding them, the Dawson City Nuggets trudged down the main street of Whitehorse. They might have walked the entire length of the street unnoticed, all the way to the Whitehorse Hotel, if Albert Forrest, their young goaltender, hadn't been leading them in song. Hoarse voices sang out "She'll Be Comin' Round the Mountain When She Comes" and "Bicycle Built For Two". They were breaking into "Auld Lang Syne" in celebration of the New Year, just two days off, when doors began to open. Curious residents stepped out onto the wooden boardwalks, anxious to identify this strange choral group, most of whom were singing off key.

"Why, it's the Dawson City hockey players," someone shouted. "They're here at last. What a plucky group! Tell the neighbors! Get everybody out! Let's give 'em a real warm welcome."

More citizens appeared, waving and shouting hello. Dogs barked and small children popped up from nowhere, scampering in front of the travelers. Men and women left meals on the table, hurried into coats and walked alongside the group, eager for details of their trip. News of their arrival swept across town faster than news of a gold strike.

When the players reached the Whitehorse Hotel, the lobby was filling up. Guests left their rooms and hurried down the stairs. The clerk behind the desk, accustomed to grabbing thirty winks during the dinner hour, was just nodding off in his chair when he heard the commotion. His head snapped upright and he leaped up, thinking the hotel might be on fire. He demanded to know what was going on. When told the Dawson City hockey club was outside, he scurried about, checking the number of available rooms and making sure each room had a key.

He called for the cook and told him to prepare thick caribou steaks and put more potatoes in the pot; there were at least nine more diners on their way. When the first members of the team entered the lobby and stamped the snow from their boots, the clerk was composed and ready for them. He flashed a toothy smile and said, "Welcome to the Whitehorse Hotel, gentlemen. We're honored to have the next Stanley Cup champions as our guests."

Albert got the shock of his young life when he opened the blind early the next morning. He couldn't see the street below, not even when he pressed his face to the frosted glass. During the night, a light fall of snow had turned into a wind-whipped blizzard. At least a foot of snow covered everything in sight.

Albert dressed quickly and raced downstairs where several of his teammates stared glumly out the lobby window.

"Might just as well have stayed in bed," Norman Watt sighed. "None of us are going anywhere today. Just got word the train can't move. Drifts four feet high in places along the track."

"But we've got to catch the ship in Skagway," said Hector. "It's due there tomorrow and leaves the following day. If we miss the ship it may be a week before another one comes along."

"Who wants to wait here?" said Gloomy Johnstone. "This place is colder than a hangman's heart."

The men spent all of one day and most of a second waiting for the storm to blow itself out. While they were waiting they shoveled off a patch of ice and played a game of hockey against a local team. But in minutes the ice was covered with snow again, and they were forced to give up.

Finally, the storm moved off to the east, the railway tracks were cleared of drifting snow and they heard the welcome shriek of the train whistle. It was the engineer's signal to grab their belongings and climb aboard. The train was leaving for Skagway.

There was another delay when they reached the U.S. border east of Skagway. Customs and immigration officials wanted a little chat with the players before allowing them to proceed. "Frankly, boys, we never expected you to show up," one of the customs agents said to Albert. "We heard you were coming but we figured heck, those boys will see all this snow and head right back to Dawson as fast as they can go."

"Not us," said Albert, "Most of us had to suffer some hardship getting into the Klondike and now we're having a rough time getting out. But we're a team and there's not a quitter on it. We're determined to get to Ottawa. Isn't that right, fellows?"

The players cheered Albert's little speech and Hector said, "You notice, fellows, how young Albert's come out of his shell and speaks right up now. What happened to that shy little fellow who was all tongue-tied when we first named him to the team?"

Everyone laughed and Albert felt himself blushing. But it was true. Albert had learned to speak up in the last few days. He was changing and learning things about himself all the time. He was even beginning to think that someday he might be a leader on this team, not merely a follower.

"So we're in United States territory now," stated Norman Smith, as the train rattled on toward Skagway.

"That's right, Norman," said Albert, putting down the book he was reading. "And it's a huge territory, isn't it? But so far away from the rest of the nation that it may never become a state. I borrowed this book about Alaska from a passenger in the next car. Do you know a lot of Americans don't think this great land up here is even worth holding onto? They think the United States should never have bought it from the Russians in the first place."

"Is that how they got it?" asked Norman.

"Sure. Over a hundred years ago, a Russian fur-trading company had a monopoly on the land. It was called Russian America then. About forty years ago, a man named Seward . . . I think he was the U.S. Secretary of State . . . made a deal with the Russians. He offered them seven and a half million dollars for Alaska."

"That's a heap of money," said Norman. "For land you can't grow anything on. You ever try to grow corn under three feet of snow, Albert? Or a row of tomatoes? Seems to me the Russians got the best of that deal."

"A lot of Americans think that way," said Albert. "Or used to. But the purchase price worked out to only a fifth of a penny an acre. Seems to me that's a real bargain. Maybe you can't grow tomatoes here. I don't know. But look at all the gold they've discovered in Alaska. And think of how much more may be waiting to be discovered. Then there's the lumbering and the fishing and the fur business. Heck, maybe someday people will pay good money just to come up here and look around, to see how beautiful it is and to see what they got for their money."

Norman snorted. "Nobody is ever going to come up here just to have a look-see," he said. "It's too dern cold for most people, if you ask me."

"Well, I love the north country," said Albert. "I can't ever see myself living anywhere else."

"Then you're a rare bird, Albert," replied Norman. "You know, don't you, that most of us on the Nuggets can't wait to get outside again. You've heard about the gold running out in Dawson and how it's time to pick up stakes. You must know that when the games are over in Ottawa most of us won't be coming back to the Yukon. You know that, don't you, kid?"

"Yes," said Albert. "Yes, I guess I know that, Norman." He stared out the window. But when he thought about it, he really hadn't known it at all.

When the train pulled into Skagway, local residents on the station platform were forced to leap nimbly aside as several young men carrying heavy packs jumped off the train and dashed toward the harbor.

"Is she still there?" one of the young men asked an oldtimer standing on the dock. "Is the *Amur* still in port?"

"No, she's not," replied the oldtimer, puffing on his pipe. "Sailed a couple of hours ago, she did. Captain said he couldn't wait any longer for a hockey team that should have been here days ago."

"I know that captain," Albert said, thinking of the agonizing moments when the honeymoon couple fell off the deck of the *Amur* years earlier. "The man's a heartless so-and-so. Not the kind of fellow who'd wait for anyone."

"Is there another ship coming in?" someone asked the oldtimer.

"Well, the *Romano*'s on her way. She'll be here in a day or two. Then she sails back to Seattle."

"Seattle! But we want to go to Vancouver," cried Sureshot Kennedy. "If we get to Seattle it'll take us another day to get back over the border and up to Vancouver. We'll never get to Ottawa at this rate."

"That's right," said Norman. "Our schedule is shot to pieces again. We're stranded here in Skagway and there's not a dern thing we can do about it.

10

A Narrow Escape

Albert loved the smell of the ocean. One day while the hockey players were still waiting for a ship, he was strolling along the beach in Skagway, skipping flat stones across the water, when he encountered an old sailor sitting on a log and whittling on a piece of white wood.

"How do, son," the sailor said, grinning at Albert. "Say, do you have a match, by chance. My dern pipe's gone out."

"Sorry," Albert replied. "I don't smoke so I have no matches."

"No matter," laughed the sailor, "Pipe-smokin' is a nasty habit anyway. But it helps to pass the time when an old salt like me is away on a long voyage." He patted the log beside him. "Sit down and we'll chat a spell."

Albert liked the old man and soon found himself talking about his trip from Dawson, how he longed to be on his way to Ottawa where he would play for the Stanley Cup and how frustrating it was to be in Skagway with nothing to do.

"We found a small patch of ice to practice on yesterday," Albert said, "But the ice was so thin our skates cut right through into the sand and gravel underneath. I'm afraid we're going to be in terrible condition for the series in Ottawa. And there's still no sign of our ship, the *Romano*."

"I know all about ships," the old man replied. "Been sailin' on them all my life." And he proceeded to tell Albert some tales of the sea. He talked about whaling expeditions to the Arctic seas. He talked of shipwrecks and storms and mutinous crews. He gazed out to sea and talked about "the wonders of the deep" and how a sailor's life "was a man's life, full of adventure and excitement."

Albert was impressed with his new friend.

"Look out to sea, lad," the old man said, pointing a gnarled hand toward the bay. "That's my ship out there riding at anchor. The *Nellie Glenn*. Ain't she a beauty? Say, how'd you like to come aboard and meet my mates? We're sailing north tomorrow, off chasing whales again. But we've got plenty of time today. And the crew would love to meet a young fellow who's going to play for the Stanley Cup. How about it? I'll have you back on shore in jig time."

Albert agreed to accompany the old sailor on a visit to the *Nellie Glenn*. They rowed out to the ship in a small skiff and after climbing a rope ladder, they were hoisted onto the deck by a couple of husky young seamen.

Albert was given a tour of the ship from "stem to gudgeon" as the old sailor described it. Then he was introduced to the captain. Captain Farrell squeezed Albert's hand and said, "Well, you're not very big are you, boy? But sometimes little men make the best sailors. Any interest in going to sea, boy?"

Albert told Captain Farrell he'd never given much thought to a sailing life. "I got awful seasick the first time," he added, "when my family booked passage from Vancouver to Skagway on our way to the gold fields."

"Almost everybody gets seasick if they're not used to rough seas," said the captain, throwing an arm around Albert's shoulder. "But you'll get over it. After a day or two aboard the *Nellie Glenn* you'll find your sea legs and be just like the rest of us."

"Wait, sir," Albert said, slipping out from under the captain's arm. "You don't understand. I'm not here to join your crew. I'm just visiting your ship."

Sensing danger, Albert glanced toward the distant shore. It was deserted. He thought of his teammates back at the hotel. They had no idea where he was. He wished he'd told them he was going for a walk on the beach.

53

Albert fought back his fear and took a step toward the ship's rail. But when he moved, the captain nodded at some nearby sailors and they started forward, forming a loose circle around Albert.

"I'm afraid we've got you now, lad," the captain grinned, showing crooked teeth. "We're about to haul anchor and go whaling. You can be our new cabin boy. Some people will claim we shanghaied you but I call it giving you a chance, a chance to see the wonders of the deep, a chance to be a sailor."

He turned to his crew. "Ain't that right, boys?"

The sailors laughed and said in unison, "That's right, captain."

Captain Farrell took a roll of bills from his pocket and tucked the money into the old man's shirt pocket and said, "Nice job, old salt. Nobody can touch you for sweet-talkin' an innocent young man into comin' aboard the *Nellie Glenn*."

Albert knew he must act quickly. If he delayed a moment longer he'd be locked in a cabin below until the ship was miles out to sea.

He forced himself to smile disarmingly at the crew. Then he said, "Well, the joke's on me, fellows. Since I have no choice, I'll make the best of this situation. Of course, I'll be your cabin boy. And I look forward to going off sailing with you."

He turned to the old man who'd lured him aboard the *Nellie Glenn*. "No hard feelings, mister. I know you were just following orders."

He smiled his best smile at the old man and moved as if to shake his hand. But when he stepped forward, he looked beyond the old sailor to the ship's rigging, leading to the masts above.

The sailors, thrown off guard by Albert's reaction, were surprised by what happened next. Albert shouldered the old man aside, leaped for the rigging, and began climbing up the ropes. He heard shouts from below. The captain cried out angrily, "Catch that boy! Throw him in chains!"

Albert felt a strong hand catch him by the boot but he wriggled free, leaving his boot behind. He flew up the rigging, higher and higher. Above him, he could see a small platform, a place where sailors were posted as lookouts when the ship was far from land, a place where whalers could easily spot the huge mammals they pursued so relentlessly.

Albert thought fleetingly of the terror a whale must feel when the harpoon pierced its thick skin. And he tried hard to fight back his own fears now that he'd become the whalers' human quarry.

When Albert reached the platform, he looked down. A sailor was coming up fast. The sailor looked Albert in the eye and said, "Now what're you gonna do, boy? Come on down like a good little man."

Albert shook his head.

"Then I'll have to drag you down," the sailor said, his voice turning to a snarl.

He placed one hand on the edge of the platform and prepared to heave himself up next to Albert. But Albert still had one booted foot and he brought his heel down on the sailor's knuckles. The sailor screamed and would have fallen if two of his mates hadn't caught him as he lost his balance.

"Why, you little devil," the sailor snarled at Albert. "I'll whip you within an inch of your life when I get you below."

"No, you'll not whip me. You'll not catch me, either," Albert yelled back. "And I'm not going whaling with ugly men like you."

And with that, Albert stood on the very edge of the platform. He looked down once, then closed his eyes and leaped into space. The shouts of his pursuers ceased as Albert's slim body flashed through the air in a graceful dive.

Someone shouted, "Look out below! He'll hit the deck."

But Albert's athletic skills served him well. He soared just beyond the ship's rail, plummeted into the frigid water and disappeared from sight.

Albert was accustomed to cold water. In the spring of the year, he and his friends in Dawson often went skinny-dipping in the frigid waters of the nearby streams. But he'd never felt water this cold. He knew he must persevere. If he gave in to the urge to come to the surface, he'd be captured. The thought of being locked up aboard the *Nellie Glenn* forced him to swim deeper.

He opened his eyes and found himself close to the ship's hull. Using one hand to follow the contours of the hull, he went down, down, down. Then he twisted his body under the hull and swam swiftly up the other side. He prayed the sailors would remain on the side of the ship where he'd entered the water. He envisioned them waiting for him to surface so they could pluck him from the sea. Perhaps they'd think he'd struck his head and drowned. If they stayed where they were, he still had a chance.

Albert saw a shadow above him. It was the small skiff the old man had used to bring him out to the *Nellie Glenn*. Albert popped to the surface and glanced up at the rail of the ship. There was no one there. His teeth were chattering. Surely, somebody will hear me, he thought. Then he was in the skiff, and with trembling hands he untied the simple knot holding the skiff to the *Nellie Glenn*. He slipped the oars into the oarlocks and pointed the skiff toward shore.

Rowing quickly, he began to count. If he could count to twenty before the sailors discovered him, he might get away.

One . . . two . . . three . . . four . . .

Albert reached a count of sixteen before he was spotted by the sailors on board.

"There he is! After him, boys. Get another skiff in the water."

Albert rowed even faster. He was halfway to shore before the crew of the *Nellie Glenn* set off in pursuit.

But Albert was certain they'd never catch up. He was in splendid physical shape and already his body was warming up because of the hard rowing. His little skiff knifed through the water and the sailors from the whaling ship soon gave up the chase. One of the sailors stood up in the bow and shook his fist at Albert. Albert waved back and laughed. He stopped rowing for a moment and shouted at his pursuers through cupped hands, "I told you I wasn't going whaling with you. But thanks for asking me, anyway."

He felt the bottom of the skiff grinding gently against the small pebbles on the beach. Then Albert was off along the beach, water squishing from his remaining boot, the pebbles cold and hard under his bare foot. Soon he was on the board-walk leading into town.

My teammates will never believe me when I tell them what happened, he thought. They'll never believe how close I came to being shanghaied.

He glanced back and saw the *Nellie Glenn* raising sail. Captain Farrell's in a hurry to clear the harbor, Albert thought. He's afraid I'll come back with the authorities. He wants as much ocean between the *Nellie Glenn* and Skagway as possible.

That's as close as I want to come to seeing the wonders of the deep, Albert snorted, thinking of the old sailor's description of a seafaring life.

Well, that adventure cost me a good soaking and I've lost a boot, he reflected. But it might have cost me a lot more, like a chance to play for the Stanley Cup. If I hadn't been able to wriggle out of a desperate situation it might even have cost me my life.

He smiled. Imagine that old sailor fooling me with his smooth talk, he said to himself. What a gullible fellow I am. Life is certainly full of surprises.

11

To Seattle and Vancouver

"What an ugly old ship she is," said Albert, when he first saw the rust-covered *SS Romano*. "Looks like she's ready for a ships' graveyard."

"It's true she's no beauty," admitted Hector Smith. "But what do we care? Besides, we're all so tired we'll be sacked out in a bunk all the way to Seattle. We'll sleep like babes all the way."

"I feel sorry for any of you fellows who get seasick," chuckled Sureshot Kennedy. "I've never had that problem myself. I guess I'm just a natural born sailor. Looks like I'll have to eat all the good food you boys'll be too ill to feast on." He laughed aloud and talked about the many sea voyages he'd taken. "And never any ill effects," he added.

Soon the *Romano*, twisting and groaning as if reluctant to face the threatening waves beyond the harbor, was rolling and pitching in heavy seas. Most of her passengers staggered about, sick to their stomachs, regretting the moment they'd set foot on the ship.

Albert, between trips to the rail, lay on his bunk, moaning and perspiring, wondering when his stomach would next betray him. He envied Sureshot Kennedy, who bragged of never having been seasick. Moments later, holding his mouth, Albert ran for the deck. There he saw a familiar figure draped over the rail. It was Sureshot, heaving and snorting and cursing each passing wave. When he saw Albert's stare, Sureshot gasped, "It's not what you're thinkin', boy. I'm not bein' seasick. It's just a touch of the flu, is what it is. I've never been seasick in my life." Albert had to grin in spite of his queasy stomach.

At last, after six of the most agonizing days of his life, having lost several pounds from his thin body, Albert awoke to shouts and ringing bells. He scrambled on deck in time to see the *Romano* turn her ugly snout toward the entrance of Seattle harbor.

"Come on, Albert," shouted Hector. "Grab your gear. The ship is docking and we've a train to catch. Next stop – Vancouver."

On the train, Albert bought a Seattle paper and was surprised to see a story on the sports page about the Nuggets. The writer lauded the courage of the players and called their trek to Ottawa in quest of the Stanley Cup "a remarkable odyssey even though it holds little promise of success." The writer added:

Not only will the Yukoners lack conditioning at the end of their long journey but they are saddled with a broth of a boy in goal, a lad named Albert Forrest. Young Forrest is green as a shamrock and will soon know the feeling of a condemned man facing a firing squad when he attempts to guard his goal against the likes of one-eyed Frank McGee and his Ottawa teammates.

Albert tried to shrug off the story. He pretended he wasn't upset by it but Hector Smith saw that he was depressed and tried to cheer him up.

"Albert, you are going to find out in life, and especially in the sporting world, that people are going to write and talk about you. Don't take that writer's words as fact. It's simply his opinion that you are too young to deliver the goods. But your teammates don't feel that way. We have confidence in you. And I know that you have a lot of faith in your own ability. If you're going to make any kind of a mark in life at all, there are always going to be people around to take potshots at you. Just ignore them and never let them destroy your belief in yourself."

In Vancouver, after eighteen days of heading in every direction but east, the Nuggets found themselves settled in a private railroad car on the train bound for Ottawa.

"Whoo-oooo," howled Sureshot Kennedy, imitating the sound of the engineer's gloomy whistle as the train made its way through the mountain passes. "Whoo-oooo. I'm feelin' better boys. At last we're pointing in the right direction. Look out, Silver Seven. Here come the Nuggets."

Albert couldn't believe they had a car all to themselves.

"Colonel Boyle is paying for it," he was told by Randy McLennan. "It's costing him a fortune, forty-five dollars a day, but he said he wants us to travel in comfort and style."

"He also said he wants us to do our exercises every day so we'll be in good shape to meet the Ottawas," said Sureshot Kennedy. "But all we can do is skip rope and lift a few weights in the smoking compartment."

Mr. Templeton, the gray-haired conductor who'd welcomed them all aboard, told Albert the journey would take about five days and he promised there would be many interesting sights along the way.

"It's a wonderful way to see the country we live in," Mr. Templeton said.

He was right.

Albert remembered very little of his previous trip across the nation. He recalled being ill with the flu for most of the journey and how it had rained or snowed almost every day. So he hadn't really seen very much out the train window.

This time he marveled at the sights. His eyes feasted on the spectacular beauty of the Rocky Mountains. He saw fantastic glaciers, dark, mysterious canyons and sparkling waterfalls plunging into pools of blue-green water. He saw the turbulent Fraser River, tossing foam high in the air on its mad rush to the sea.

Mr. Templeton told him the Canadian Pacific line had been completed a few years earlier, in 1896.

"Across the continent in ninety-seven hours, Albert," Mr. Templeton had said with obvious pride. "No other railway in North America can boast of such a trip. Not one that reaches from ocean to ocean and on the same company's rails. And without a change of cars."

With the purple shadows of the Rocky Mountains all around him, Albert felt like he was in the middle of a maze. He imagined how difficult it must have been to build the railroad. He pictured the tracklayers working on the roadbed. He could hear the rumble of dynamite echoing in the canyons and high along the cliffs. He marveled at the skills of the men who drilled and blasted through solid rock to form long tunnels. He admired the boldness of the planners who laid the tracks out in long sweeping loops, up and down steep grades and over lofty stilted trestles.

As the train pressed steadily onward, the mountain ranges grew more gentle, until finally the rocky maze released the determined locomotive, allowing it to glide down gradual slopes and roll on into vast expanses of grassland.

The piercing whistle of the train seemed to signal a sigh of relief, as if it knew the most difficult part of its long journey was over. Hundreds of miles of flat land lay ahead. Now the engine leaped forward, eager to follow the gleaming rails that stretched eastward across the vast prairies, over the nation's richest grazing lands.

There was so much to see. Crystal-clear lakes tucked into groves of aspen, pastoral valleys wedged into the prairie floor, places called badlands with eerie shapes and contours caused by centuries of erosion.

He saw an Indian teepee with smoke curling from a hole at the top. He saw cowboys on horseback. The cattle they herded stared solemnly at the passing train but the cowboys hooted and hollered and waved their wide-brimmed hats at the passengers.

Albert envied the cowboys. How exciting it must be to ride a galloping horse and round up cattle, he thought. And what fun to sleep under the stars and listen to a coyote's mournful howl in the distance!

He wondered if the cowboys would envy him if they knew he was a hockey player, one of the Dawson City Nuggets, off to Ottawa to play in the Stanley Cup series. Would they have even heard of the Stanley Cup? Would they have ever experienced the joy of playing hockey themselves?

Albert wondered, if he had the chance, would he trade places with them? He turned away from the window and thought about it for a moment.

No, I would not, he decided. I rather like being Albert Forrest.

12

Albert Finds a Friend

Albert was writing in his diary when Mr. Templeton leaned over him. "Albert, come with me," he smiled. "I want you to meet someone."

Albert followed Mr. Templeton into the next car. Before he moved down the aisle, the friendly conductor turned to Albert and said, "It occurred to me that there are two young people on my train roughly the same age. I thought it would be nice if they got to know each other. I think they may have a lot in common. One is you, Albert. The other is the daughter of a friend of mine. She's going to Ottawa too."

"She?" Albert said.

"Yes, Caroline Peters. Her father is a Member of Parliament from Vancouver. She's going to visit him for a holiday. Her father asked me to take good care of her on this trip as she's traveling alone. But she has no one her own age to talk to. Would you like to meet her?"

"Well, I guess so," said Albert, although he wasn't really sure that he would. Albert was shy around girls and couldn't think when he'd ever spent much time talking to one.

Moments later, he found himself sitting across from the prettiest, most charming teenage girl he'd ever seen. Mr. Templeton turned out to be right. Caroline and Albert did have a lot in common. They both enjoyed the same subjects in school. They were both involved in sports (Caroline was a skier and belonged to a snowshoe club) and they both liked to talk about the future of Canada.

Albert thought the most attractive feature about Caroline was her smile. It was captivating. Later, in his bunk, he would write in his diary:

> I met a very pretty girl today. She has the nicest smile I've ever seen. I thought I would be shy and tongue-tied with her but I wasn't. We had fun and I lost track of time. At dinner, my teammates wondered where I'd been all afternoon. I told them I'd felt the need of some exercise so I'd jumped off the train and run along beside it for fifty or sixty miles. Hadn't they seen me out the window?
>
> They laughed at my silly answer. I'm beginning to think they like me even though some of them feel I'm going to be the weak link on the Nuggets. If only I don't let them down in the games ahead . . .

By the time the train rolled through Saskatchewan and Manitoba, Albert and Caroline were the best of friends. She wanted to know all about his life in the Yukon.

"Are there Eskimos in Dawson, Albert? And do they really live in little round huts made of ice and snow?"

He laughed. "No, there are Indians in the Klondike but Eskimos live much farther north. And yes, they do live in ice houses called igloos."

"What about polar bears? Have you ever seen one?"

"Not yet. They live farther north too. But there are plenty of other kinds of bears around Dawson. The most dangerous is the grizzly. Dad and I were prospecting up a small stream one day when we saw two cubs playing in the grass. Did we run! Jumped in our canoe and took off before the mother bear came along."

"Have you ever panned for gold using one of those funny round pans?"

"Oh, lots of times. You partly fill one of those pans with sand or gravel from a stream-bed and let the water flow over it gently while you rotate the pan. Gold is heavier than the sand or gravel so little pieces of gold are left in the bottom of the pan. There's usually a little pocket there to collect them while the lighter parts of gravel are washed away."

"Is it fun?"

"It is in the beginning. And it's really exciting to find a small nugget in your pan. A nugget is the rarest form of gold. But mostly it's just a lot of hard work."

Caroline asked about the long winters and he told her about the big blizzard that almost buried their log house the winter before last. He remembered a week when the temperatures fell to -50 and stayed there. One oldtimer warned Albert never to leave shelter if the temperature dropped any lower, for then there was danger of frosted lungs. "But it seldom gets that cold," he added. "I think it's the best place in the world to live. And you should see some of the characters we have in the Klondike."

He mentioned some of the gold seekers he'd met, men with names like Two-Step Louie, Billy the Horse and Spare-Rib Jimmy. He told her there were women named Limejuice Lil and Diamond-Tooth Gertie.

"There's even a man in Dawson who's so skinny they call him the Evaporated Kid," Albert chuckled.

Caroline leaned toward him and said, "Do you know, Albert, I almost got to see it all. When I was quite small my family set out for the gold fields. But we had to turn back. People said you could collect gold off the streets in Dawson City in those days. But that wasn't true, was it?"

Albert laughed. "Not true. All we collected off the streets in those days was mud. There was mud everywhere. My brothers and I were always getting stuck in it. If your family had reached Dawson and started a good hand laundry they'd have made more money than most of the miners."

"I remember being in a tent near a huge mountain," Caroline said. "Suddenly, people were screaming and there was snow everywhere. My uncle died there that day, trapped under an avalanche. They say I almost died too. So my father decided to return home. He lost all his life savings on that trip and had to start all over again."

"Lots of people lost their lives in the avalanches," Albert said. "And all of their money trying to get to the gold fields. And families broke up. I've been separated from my sister Evelyne for years because she was too young to travel up there with us."

He told Caroline all about Evelyne and how anxious he was to see her again. "There's a possibility Colonel Boyle will arrange some exhibition games for the Nuggets after the Stanley Cup series. I hope one of the games will be in Three Rivers."

Eventually, Albert's teammates discovered him sitting with Caroline, laughing at something one of them had said.

Albert received quite a kidding when he returned to the Nuggets' pullman. But he took the jibes of his teammates in stride. He was grateful when Randy McLennan drew him aside and said, "Albert, the fellows wouldn't kid you if they didn't like you. Remember, most of them wish they were seventeen again and had your good looks and winning smile. And by the way, if you want a teammate's opinion, your friend Caroline is a lovely-looking girl. So take my advice. Enjoy the rest of the trip with your new friend."

So Albert simply smiled when his teammates called him "Romeo" and "little heartbreaker". He ignored their comments. The hours flew by as he and Caroline got better acquainted.

She promised to come and see him play for the Stanley Cup.

"I'm sure my father will get tickets. He's a real hockey fan," she said. "And we'll persuade him to give us a tour of the Parliament Buildings. Government is very interesting, don't you think? We can sit in the gallery and watch the members debating."

The train skirted the rugged shoreline north of Lake Superior, racing through dark corridors of pine and spruce. Then it swept into the Ottawa Valley, following the winding rails that took it through the lumber towns of Pembroke and Renfrew. Soon it would deposit the Nuggets in the nation's capital.

On their final morning aboard the train, in the smoking compartment, the Nuggets were shaving faces, brushing hair, and shining shoes. They wanted to look their best when the train pulled into the Ottawa Station.

"One thing is certain," Norman Watt said as he expertly removed a budding mustache from his upper lip with a flick of his razor. "The Ottawa players will be in the best condition of their lives for this series. I hear they've been having long practices every day."

"They have a lot of pride," added Randy McLennan. "And no wonder. They have the best record of any team in hockey history. They've held the Stanley Cup for three straight years, turning back all challengers. You can bet they don't want to lose it to some unknowns from the Klondike."

Albert examined his face in the mirror. There was no need to shave since he had nothing to scrape off. Sometimes he wondered if he was ever going to grow facial hair like his teammates.

"Aw, they're not going to lose the cup," muttered Gloomy Johnstone, wiping shaving cream from his earlobe. Johnstone had earned his nickname because he seldom smiled and was sour about most things in life. He turned away from the big mirror to face the others. "Let's face it, fellows. We don't have much chance to win, do we? Look at us. Traveling all this way without being able to practice. Three of our boys still have blistered feet from walking out to Whitehorse. Then we were all sick on that old scow to Seattle. And where's Weldy Young, our best player and coach? He's days behind us if he's on his way at all."

Johnstone, catching Albert's eye in the mirror, turned to him. "Now don't take offense at this, Albert, but I'll say this to your face. You are an untried goalie, the youngest goalie ever to play in such an important series. We all know goalie is the toughest position to play and you just took it up a few weeks ago. For us to win with you in goal is, well, it's gonna take a miracle."

There was silence in the room. The others were surprised at Johnstone's outburst. Albert could feel his cheeks redden. Obviously, Gloomy Johnstone didn't have any confidence in Albert's ability as a goalie. And he thought the Nuggets' quest for the Stanley Cup was hopeless.

Albert looked Gloomy Johnstone right in the face. Then he said softly, "It really upsets me, Johnstone, to hear that you're ready to give up on the Stanley Cup before we even get a chance to play for it. It's true we've had some problems. And our chances will be badly hurt if Weldy Young doesn't show up in time. It's also true that I'm young, the youngest goalie ever to play in a Cup series. I've got no experience but you all knew that from the start. I can't promise you I'll stop the Ottawas. All I can promise you is that I'll play the very best I can. If we all play our best, why can't we upset the Silver Seven? Maybe we'll catch them napping, over confident. Isn't it better to keep a positive attitude than to admit we're beaten before we ever put our skates on?"

"Young Albert's right," said Hector Smith. "Anything can happen in sport. Look what Albert did in the skating races in Dawson. Nobody thought he could whip all those older boys. But he did."

Albert's plea for a more positive attitude gave the Nuggets something to think about as they left for the dining car. But how long will that confidence last, Albert wondered, if I let in some soft goals early in the first game of the series?

Later, Albert wrote in his diary:

> I find it interesting that my opinion of certain teammates keeps changing. Back in Dawson, I admired all of them because of their skills on the ice and because they were all so much more grownup than I was.
>
> Now I see that most of them are just ordinary fellows. There are one or two I really admire, like Randy McLennan who has studied hard to become a doctor. He is very considerate and is always there to lend a helping hand or a word of advice. There's Hector and Norman. They always treat me like an equal. They can be relied on.
>
> But one or two of my teammates disappoint me. Most

nights on the train, they've played noisy card games with strangers, rough-looking men they met somewhere along the way. I don't think they should invite these strangers back to our pullman for their games, but they do.

Last night I couldn't sleep because of the noise. I got up and saw them in the smoking compartment. I saw clouds of cigar smoke and heard plenty of strong language and laughter. They were sitting at a table covered with bottles and they were betting large amounts of money on each hand.

Gloomy Johnstone looked up from his cards and saw me standing in the doorway. He shouted in a slurred voice, "Go back to bed, Albert. You'll need plenty of rest if you're going to face the Silver Seven in a couple of days."

I shouted back, "I'd be able to sleep if you and your noisy friends would clear out of here. It's after three o'clock. And don't talk to me about facing the Silver Seven. What kind of shape are you going to be in when it comes to stopping Ottawa?"

The card players turned and stared at me. None of them said another word, not even Gloomy. I think they were amazed that a young fellow had lectured them the way a coach might have.

I glared at them for a moment. Then I went back to bed and tried to sleep.

13

The Challengers Arrive

The train chugged slowly into the Ottawa Station as if it was drained of energy after a long and difficult journey. There was a large gathering on hand to greet the passengers. Dozens of Ottawa sportsmen turned out to welcome the hockey players from the far-off Yukon.

Albert's emotions were pulling him in two directions. He wanted to be with Caroline when the passengers stepped down. He knew she wanted him to meet her father. On the other hand, he felt he should be with his teammates. When he explained his dilemma to Caroline she smiled and said, "Just do what you think is best, Albert."

He decided to step down with his teammates when the train pulled in, not because he wanted his share of the attention the visiting players were bound to get, but because he felt he belonged to this team. He was one of the Dawson City Nuggets and he was proud of it. This was one occasion when he should be with his teammates. He was certain Caroline would understand.

Colonel Boyle was there to greet them. He stood out from the crowd, his large frame covered by an expensive sealskin coat. He had rushed to Ottawa from a business meeting in Detroit, arriving moments earlier, just in time to greet the hockey players whose trip he'd financed.

He was joined on the platform by officials from the Ottawa Hockey Club. There was a great cheer as the Nuggets stepped down from their car and there were handshakes all around. Colonel Boyle had a few words for each of his players. When he noticed Albert hanging back, he stepped forward and pumped the young goalie's hand until Albert winced. He said, "Good to have you with us, lad. Good luck against the Ottawas."

Fortunately for Albert, there was a delay while the players' bags were unloaded. Albert seized the opportunity to run down the platform looking for Caroline. He found her on the arm of the most distinguished-looking man Albert had ever seen. He was a tall man with a pleasant face almost hidden by a bushy black beard.

Caroline's face lit up when she saw Albert. "Come and meet my father," she said. Mr. Peters shook hands with Albert and told him he was looking forward to seeing the games against the Silver Seven.

Albert had said little more than, "I'm pleased to meet you, sir," when he heard his teammates calling his name.

"C'mon, Albert. We're off to our hotel. Everybody is waiting for you."

As he ran back along the platform Caroline called after him, "I'll see you at the game, Albert. Good luck!" He looked back. She waved a gloved hand and smiled. His heart gave a little flip.

Horse-drawn sleighs were ready to whisk the players to the nearby Russell Hotel. Albert leaped aboard the last sleigh and noticed his teammates grinning at him. "Oh, oh," he said, starting to get up, "I've left my bag on the platform."

Hector Smith put a hand out, restraining him. "Just relax, young Albert," he said. "Your bag is safely aboard."

"It is? Gee, thanks a lot, Hector. Did you put it there?"

"No, Cupid did," Hector said, winking at the others.

The next morning at breakfast, the Nuggets were the center of attention. Waiters and busboys fussed over them. Small schoolboys peeked through the frosted windows of the hotel dining hall, hoping to catch a glimpse of the Stanley Cup challengers.

Colonel Boyle arranged practice time at the Ottawa Arena

and told the Nuggets that all games in the series were sold out. On the way to practice he stopped at a store and bought them new uniforms. The players voted for dark blue jerseys with gold trim and white pants. Each player selected a new stick. Albert was delighted with his goal stick. It was slightly wider in the shaft than the other sticks. It was the first new stick he'd ever owned and it cost fifty cents. Colonel Boyle told him to take good care of the stick because he'd be needing it in the exhibition games he'd booked to follow the series with the Silver Seven.

"Will we be playing in Three Rivers, Colonel Boyle?" Albert asked. "My sister Evelyne lives there. I haven't seen her in years."

"I don't think so, Albert. I've booked several games in the Maritimes and a couple in Pittsburgh. But none in Three Rivers. Not so far."

Albert was bitterly disappointed.

Colonel Boyle had arranged for a team photo. Outside Dey's Arena the photographer positioned the players in two rows with Colonel Boyle sitting in the middle of the first row. The Nuggets, in their new uniforms, looked splendid, and everyone laughed when Norman said, "Someone paint a mustache on Albert so he'll look as old as the rest of us."

Despite the fast ice in the arena, the players weren't pleased with the results of their practice. They felt sluggish and awkward. They'd been away from hockey too long. Their passes were erratic and their shooting weak. And they tired quickly. When they trooped into the dressing room huffing and puffing, Colonel Boyle gave them some bad news.

"Men, I pleaded with the Ottawa management for a postpone-ment of the series. I told them you boys were exhausted from your long journey. Give us a day or two to get ready, I pleaded, let us get our skating legs back. But they just laughed at me and said no. So, like it or not, the series begins tomorrow night."

"Colonel Boyle, is there any word from Weldy?" someone asked. "We were lost out there in practice without him. We've always relied on Weldy to run the show."

"Not a word, I'm afraid," answered Colonel Boyle. "We know he left the Yukon almost three weeks ago. Let's just hope he shows up on the afternoon train tomorrow."

14

The Series Begins

When the Nuggets skated out to warm up for the first game of their best-of-three series with the Ottawas, their best player was still missing. Weldy Young was somewhere between Dawson and Ottawa and the Nuggets would have to get along without him.

Albert was excited as he took his place in the Nuggets' goal but he noticed some of his teammates were circling the ice with slumped shoulders and long faces. They should be eager to play, Albert thought. What's wrong with them? Didn't they receive a fine ovation from the fans when they skated out? Albert knew what was troubling them. They don't think we can win without Weldy, he realized. Why, they're skating around like they've got lead in their britches.

"C'mon, fellows, let's move!" Albert pleaded, banging his stick on the ice. "Let's take it right to the Ottawas."

But his teammates didn't seem to hear. Most of them cast anxious glances down the ice where the Ottawas were energetically warming up. Buzzing around the ice in their famous barber-pole sweaters were some of hockey's greatest stars: Art Moore, Harvey Pulford, Alf Smith and one-eyed Frank McGee. McGee was called "the greatest player in the world" by his fans.

Before the opening faceoff, Colonel Boyle called the Nuggets to the bench.

"Randy, you'll have to be the team leader in place of Weldy. You make most of the coaching decisions," he directed. "I'll stay behind the bench and help out as best I can."

A great cheer went up when the Governor-General, Lord Grey, moved to center ice and dropped the puck to get the series underway. While the Governor-General was being escorted back to his private box, Albert spied Caroline in the crowd. She waved at him and he gave a little nod and smiled in her direction.

Then the battle was underway.

The pace of the game was frantic. The Ottawas stormed into the Nuggets' end of the rink and Albert had to turn aside three quick shots in a row. Then he made a fine save on McGee, who broke through alone.

The Nuggets took the pressure off briefly by lofting the puck down the ice and the Ottawas chased back for it.

Here they come again, thought Albert, and he braced himself between the two posts. A hard shot by Pulford hit him on the ankle. Another by Smith struck his goal stick. Westwick almost tucked the puck into the corner but Albert knocked it away at the last second.

Albert's teammates appeared to be paralyzed. They couldn't catch the fleet Ottawa players and, when they did, they were pushed aside or knocked down.

"Come on, fellows, get in the game," Albert shouted. "Don't let them barrel through like that."

Finally, Norman Watt, who'd been bowled over three times by Ottawa's tough forward, Alf Moore, had had enough. He steamed into Moore. Watt's stick flew up and Moore crumpled to the ice with blood streaming from his head. Watt was given a five-minute penalty.

With the rugged Watt off the ice, the Ottawas stormed in again. And finally, after Albert had made a half dozen brilliant saves, Westwick scored the first goal of the series.

Two minutes later, the Silver Seven scored again when the puck deflected off a defender's stick. It changed direction just as Albert moved to kick it aside. It zipped in behind him. The goal judge, standing on the ice behind Albert, waved his white handkerchief to signal the score. Two years earlier, the goal judge might have been knocked down by the flying puck. But the new goal nets, recently introduced to hockey, made his job much less dangerous.

When Watt returned from his penalty, he promptly smacked Moore again with his stick. Referee Styles said to him, "Mr. Watt, that will cost you another five minutes. You'd better start behaving yourself."

Watt scowled at the official but he did as he was told. The Ottawas scored their third goal two minutes later but not before Albert stymied them with half a dozen outstanding saves.

Now every time Albert blocked a shot or steered one sharply to the corner, he earned polite applause from the Ottawa fans. They appreciated his sparkling play. And when the Nuggets skated off at half time the fans rose to cheer him again.

During the intermission the crowd was entertained by Professor Rudolph West, who gave an exhibition of club swinging. The crowd gasped as the whirling clubs spun over the professor's bald head. Then Professor West performed a series of intricate feats with razor-sharp swords. He cut a potato in half resting in the palm of a spectator's hand, and another placed on the side of a young boy's neck. His skill was roundly applauded, except by the young boy who fainted dead away. Professor West's arm shot out and caught the lad by the back of his jacket before he hit the ice.

After Professor West bowed in all directions and left, some fans amused themselves by tossing pennies on the ice. They roared with laughter at the mad scramble that followed. Dozens of youngsters came flying out of the stands to claim the coins, slipping, sliding, pushing and sprawling in a frantic rush to grasp the rolling pennies.

If the intermission helped the Nuggets catch their breath, it did wonders for the Silver Seven. Ottawa stormed back in on Albert as soon as the puck was placed between the sticks of the opposing centers and referee Styles rang his little bell.

Albert made several magnificent saves but it was only a matter of time before the puck whistled past him once, twice, three more times.

Albert was very weary and dropped to his knees after two of the goals. Referee Styles took pity on him and delayed facing the puck until Albert struggled to his feet. "Just remember, young man," he whispered to Albert, "I'm supposed to hand out a penalty to any goalie who drops to the ice."

The Dawson players rallied briefly and a flurry of shots on the Ottawa goalie produced a pair of scores.

But the effort it took to score the goals sapped their strength. They failed to maintain the pace, and with tongues dragging, they could only watch in frustration as the Silver Seven hurled another barrage of shots at poor Albert.

The young goalie darted back and forth, deflecting, batting, stopping what looked like a blur of hockey pucks. But he couldn't turn them all aside. Before time ran out, the seventh, eighth and ninth goals eluded him. When referee Styles rang the bell to end the game, the score was Ottawa 9, Dawson 2.

Albert was so weary at game's end he could barely stand. The thin pads he wore proved to be inadequate cushions, and the hard shots he'd stopped left his limbs battered and bruised.

He skated slowly to the Dawson bench and quenched his thirst, dipping a long-handled metal cup into a bucket of cold water. His teammates sat on the low boards looking dazed and dejected. Then they rose and followed Colonel Boyle across the ice to shake hands with the victors.

The Silver Seven not only pumped Albert's hand, they pounded him on the back and told him what a fine game he'd played.

"Despite the score, that was the finest goaltending we've encountered this season," said Rat Westwick, one of the Ottawa stars. "And we've played against all the best goalies in the east."

The Governor General, after congratulating each of the winners, came over and shook hands with the losers. Then he took Albert aside and spoke to him.

"Young man, you were magnificent tonight," he said. "A very plucky performance indeed. It would be an honor to have you join us at Government House tomorrow night. My friend Mr. Peters and his daughter Caroline will be among the guests and they would like very much for you to be there."

Albert stammered his thanks and said he'd be delighted to attend, providing it was all right with Colonel Boyle.

"I have already asked Colonel Boyle for his permission," replied Lord Grey. "And it's perfectly all right with him. See you at seven tomorrow, then. And by the way, Albert, bring your skates. We've got some interesting sporting activities planned."

15

A Thrilling Race
at Government House

Early the following evening, Caroline, Albert and Mr. Peters rode to Government House in the back of a sleigh.

It had been a full day and Albert stifled a yawn. That morning the Nuggets had held a team meeting and a light practice at Dey's Arena. Most of the players were stiff and sore after the previous night's defeat.

Mr. Peters had taken Caroline and Albert to lunch and then to see the famous Rideau Canal. After that they had visited the Parliament Buildings. While Mr. Peters hurried off to his place in the House of Commons, the two teenagers found seats in the gallery. They listened attentively as members of parliament debated the important political issues of the day in the great hall below. Mr. Peters was called on to respond to a member's question and used powerful language to make his point. Then he made the members of both parties laugh at his clever and humorous remarks. Several men applauded when he was finished.

The jingling sleigh and its three occupants entered the grounds of Government House, home of Lord Grey, the Governor General, and Lady Grey.

"What a fascinating place!" Albert said.

Japanese lanterns hung everywhere, illuminating the winter landscape. On the grounds, there were toboggan slides and ski trails. A number of men and ladies on snowshoes trekked around a large frozen pond on which skaters darted and twirled.

There was a bandshell overlooking the pond and the musicians were already filling the cold night air with popular songs of the day.

The guests, and there appeared to be dozens of them, were greeted in the foyer of Government House by Lord and Lady Grey. Then proper shoes were exchanged for boots suitable for tramping through the snow. Skates and skis were supplied to guests who were encouraged to test the frozen surface of the pond and the steep slopes of the nearby hill.

Mr. Peters suggested that Caroline and Albert find some diversion to keep them busy while he wandered off to discuss politics with his parliamentary friends.

The young couple climbed hand in hand to the top of the toboggan slide and took their places on the varnished sled. Seconds later, they were hurtling down the icy run. Caroline closed her eyes and put both arms around Albert's waist. Whenever the toboggan hit a bump and threatened to toss them into the snow, she screamed in his ear and squeezed him tight.

After that they stood by the bandstand and listened to the sweet music, singing along whenever a familiar song was played.

Daisy, Daisy, give me your answer do,
I'm half crazy, all for the love of you . . .

From the top of a rise, they watched stout men with brooms sweeping a path for heavy rocks on a patch of ice set aside for curling.

Later, by the pond, Albert saw a familiar figure in the crowd. It was Frank McGee, the great star of the Silver Seven.

McGee smiled at Albert and approached him. "So we meet again, young Forrest. Here for the big skating race, are you? No, that can't be. Most goalies are very poor skaters, aren't they?"

"I don't know anything about a skating race, Mr. McGee," Albert replied.

"It doesn't matter," said McGee with a laugh, "because I plan to win it anyway. Every year at this event the Governor General donates a gold medal to the race winner. Ten laps around the pond. Any of the guests can enter but no one has ever come close to beating me. I come back each year to defend my title."

"And what title is that, sir?" Caroline asked sweetly.

Frank McGee rewarded her with a half smile, "The title of fastest man on skates, miss. I know it sounds immodest but that's what's inscribed on the gold medal. I have five of them at home and tonight I'd like to add number six to my collection."

Caroline turned to Albert. "Are you going to enter the race, Albert?"

"Well, no, I don't think . . ."

"I'm sure he'd prefer not to, miss," said McGee. "Young Forrest here is a goalie, you see, and a pretty good one. But goalies are poor skaters. That's why they become goalies. Isn't that right, Forrest? And I wouldn't want to embarrass my young friend from the Klondike tonight."

McGee chuckled and added, "Poor Forrest suffered enough last night. And with more to come tomorrow."

Albert looked McGee straight in the eye – his good eye – and said, "Mr. McGee, I happen to have my skates with me tonight. And poor skater or not, it'll be my pleasure to race against the fastest man on ice."

A few minutes later, the clanging of a bell brought all the guests to the side of the pond. The big race was about to begin. In all, there were seven contestants for Frank McGee's crown but only one or two were serious skaters. Most entered just to be able to tell their friends they'd raced against the great Frank McGee. Nobody knew what to expect from Albert, the visitor from the Yukon.

When the starter dropped his handkerchief and shouted "Go" the race was underway. The scrrrrunch, scrrrrunch, scrrrunch of sharp blades digging into hard ice could be heard across the pond. Frank McGee, his powerful legs churning, shot into the lead. Albert trailed the field. There was a long way to go and

Albert didn't want to burn himself out in the first couple of laps. Besides, he hadn't had a chance to warm up properly and he didn't want to risk an injury, like a cramp or a muscle pull.

By the end of the third lap, Albert's adrenalin was pumping. It was as if an inner voice was telling him, "Let's fly now, Albert. Let's go after McGee."

Albert tucked his arms in behind his back and leaned forward into the wind. He felt strong and fit and his confidence soared when he saw that he was closing fast on the great McGee.

With two laps to go, McGee looked back once or twice. He was breathing heavily and his stride had shortened. With fifty yards to go, he looked back again and was alarmed to see Albert moving smoothly over the ice with powerful strides, and catching up.

There was a furious dash to the finish line.

As the distance between the two swift skaters closed, Albert could see little chips of ice tossed in the air by McGee's flashing blades. Now he was even with McGee and he was forced to dodge the man's flailing elbow.

Ten yards. From some inner source Albert summoned one last burst of energy. He forged ahead of the Ottawa star and shot across the finish line, snapping a red ribbon held there by two young boys who were jumping up and down in their excitement.

McGee, in a desperate lunge to finish first, staggered and fell to the ice. He slid along on his knees for some distance, then rolled on his back and lay there, staring up at the stars, breathing hoarsely, totally spent.

Albert circled the course one more time, slowing down, then coasting, hands on his knees, pulse pounding in his ears. He could heard the crowd cheering. When he looked up, he realized the cheers were for him, for winning the race, for beating the mighty Frank McGee, for winning the Governor General's gold medal.

Caroline rushed up and hugged him. "Oh, Albert," she cried. "You did it! You beat Frank McGee. Now you're the fastest man on ice. You know, you're really quite wonderful, Albert."

Albert blushed and said, "Thank you, Caroline. I think you're wonderful, too." Then he looked beyond her. There, slumped in a snowbank, was the dejected figure of Frank McGee.

Now he knows one goalie who can skate, Albert thought. And tomorrow night, with a hockey stick in his hands, he'll have his chance to get even for tonight.

When the Governor General presented Albert with the gleaming gold medal on the steps of Government House, he told the assembled guests, "This young man has impressed us all as an outstanding athlete whose astonishing victory in the annual skating race will be talked about for years to come."

Then the Governor General put his arm around Albert's shoulder and led him indoors. "Come along," he said. "I'll give you a personal tour of this little mansion we live in."

While Albert was establishing a warm friendship with the Governor General, there was another interesting development taking place a few blocks away. A few of Albert's teammates were involved in a heated discussion with some Ottawa fans in the bar of the Russell Hotel.

The Ottawa fans boasted that their team was the finest ever assembled and their record proved it. "Why if it hadn't been for that young fellow in goal last night, the Silver Seven might have scored fifty goals," one of them claimed.

"And you haven't seen Frank McGee at his best," said another. "Young Forrest held him to one goal last night. McGee always gets three or four goals a game. Always. Wait till you see him go tomorrow."

Norman Watt was angered by the smug remarks. He stood up and said in a loud voice, "So McGee's the best you've got, is it? Well, let me tell you, boys, he didn't look so hot last night. And I don't expect we'll have much trouble holding him in check tomorrow. He's just another hockey player as far as we're concerned."

The Ottawa fans laughed and hooted. Then a man in their group jumped up, struggled into his hat and coat and headed for the door. With his hand on the doorknob, he shouted back at Norman. "I heard that, mister, and you're going to regret those words. All it takes to get Frank McGee going is for someone to insult him. When he's mad he's unstoppable. When he gets back from winning the big race at Government House tonight I'm going to tell him exactly what you said about him. Then watch him make monkeys of you fellows tomorrow."

The man stormed out into the frosty night, the door slamming behind him.

"Who was that?" Norman inquired.

"Now you boys are in the soup," chuckled the Ottawa fans. "That was Billy McGee, Frank McGee's brother."

16

The Second Game

The Nuggets' dressing room was quiet, too quiet. Skates, pads and jerseys were donned in silence. It's as if we're all going out to face a firing squad, thought Albert. Maybe we are. What we need is someone to pep us up, to inspire us. Weldy would do it but he's still not here. What a shame he didn't arrive in time.

When Albert tried to encourage his teammates by saying, "C'mon fellows, we can do it. Let's take it to them. Let's win tonight," most of the players stared at the floor, deep in their own thoughts. So Albert sat back and said no more.

Colonel Boyle entered the room bearing more bad news. "Randy McLennan can't suit up, boys," he said grimly. "His ankles are all bruised from the beating he took from the Ottawa sticks the other night. Fairbairn will play in his place."

Once again, Dey's Arena was jammed for game two of the series. The band played lively music as the fans rushed to find seats in the best locations. Lord and Lady Grey made their entrance to warm applause. His Excellency gave Albert a brief salute and Albert smiled back.

With the biggest game of his life just moments away, something unexpected happened to Albert, something that broke his concentration. When he took his place in goal, he felt something sting the back of his neck. It felt like a bee sting. He rubbed the spot and heard laughter behind him. Then he felt another sting, this time on his ear.

He spun around and saw two young lads with peashooters

melt into the crowd. Peashooters! Albert sighed and rubbed his neck. Don't tell me I'm going to have pucks flying at me from one direction and peas from another, he said to himself. The fans, sensing his frustration, simply laughed.

Referee Harlow Styles called the teams to center ice and told them to play by the rules. "No dirty tricks from any of you," he warned.

Then the game was underway.

The Nuggets went quickly to the attack and tested Ottawa goalie Finnie with one or two hard shots. But in their anxiety to open up a lead, they grew careless and Westwick broke away with McGee. Albert was helpless to stop them as some slick passing resulted in the first goal, Westwick slapping the puck past him. Seconds later, Westwick was allowed to break in again and it was 2-0 Ottawa.

The two quick goals took the starch out of the Nuggets and they sagged visibly. From the dejected looks on the faces of his mates, Albert suspected that the fireworks had just begun. How right he was! In the next few minutes he was under constant pressure and was forced to make several difficult saves.

It was obvious the Nuggets had lost heart. Already bruised and battered from the previous game, they were once again taking a lot of punishment from the Silver Seven. Fairbairn went down, knocked bow-legged by Westwick. And Johnstone limped away from a collision with McGee.

Then it was Albert who suffered an injury. He stuck out his leg to make a dazzling stop but the force of the shot cracked his ankle. He went down in a heap.

Grimacing with pain, Albert was helped to the dressing room. There a doctor removed his skate and examined the ankle. Then he declared, "The ankle bone has been badly bruised. You'd better take off your pads and call it a night, young man."

"I can't do that, doctor," said Albert, sitting up. "There's no one to take my place. I've got to get back in the game."

The doctor shrugged. "Hockey players," he snorted. "I'll never understand them. All right, young fellow, but it's your funeral."

The doctor applied some ice to the ankle and gradually the pain subsided enough for Albert to flex his foot back and forth. Then the ankle was taped and his skate pulled back on.

Referee Styles came into the room and asked if Albert was coming back. "I've declared a time out," he said, "but the crowd is getting restless."

When Albert skated back out, limping on his throbbing ankle, the fans gave him a huge ovation.

If the Ottawa fans felt a wave of sympathy for Albert, the Ottawa players did not. From the drop of the puck, they swarmed around his goal. Albert leaped in front of the flying pucks, frantically stopping them with his feet, his legs, his body, his stick. For a span of ten minutes or so, he was unbeatable. Later, people who were there said they had never seen such an exhibition of goaltending.

Of course, he couldn't keep it up. The pain in his ankle was almost unbearable and fatigue began to slow his reflexes. He continued to make excellent saves but now his moves were slower. And the puck began to find its way in behind him. The Ottawas scored once, twice, three times.

McGee did most of the damage. He dazzled the crowd with some fancy stickwork and skating. The Nuggets were powerless to stop his rushes. A dozen times he broke through with only Albert to beat.

Dizzy now and hobbled by his aching ankle, Albert faced shot after shot. McGee's accuracy was amazing. Four of his shots rattled off the goalposts before bouncing in. Albert lost track of the score. Every time he looked around, the goal judge was gleefully waving his big white hankie.

Albert remembered little of the intermission at half time. He was exhausted, frustrated and dizzy from the throbbing pain in his ankle. He lay on a bench with a cold towel over his forehead and stared up at the ceiling.

The second half was a blur. There were sights and sounds and thoughts that seemed unreal, out of focus. He saw striped sweaters coming at him from all directions. There was pain, inflicted by a hard rubber puck. There was torment, wondering when the torture would end, wondering why his teammates had caved in. And through the haze, there was the imposing figure of Frank McGee scoring goal after goal.

At last the game was over and Albert slumped to the ice. He could feel the frozen surface cold against his cheek. He could hear the crowd whistling and cheering, celebrating the Ottawa victory. He could hear the band playing. But he couldn't move. This must be what it's like to faint, he thought.

Then a remarkable thing happened. Before the Nuggets or anyone else could get to Albert, Frank McGee skated swiftly across the ice and helped the exhausted goaltender to his feet. The powerful Ottawa star lifted Albert in his arms, goal pads and all, and carried him off the ice.

By the time McGee reached the side of the rink, Albert was fully conscious so McGee gently put him down. Albert staggered but did not fall. McGee placed a strong arm around Albert's shoulder and told him he'd played a marvelous series.

Then McGee looked up at the crowd and shouted, "Give this man an ovation! He really deserves it."

Following the final game, the players and officials from both teams adjourned to the banquet hall at the Russell Hotel. After food and drink was consumed in huge quantities, it was time for speeches.

Colonel Boyle got up and praised the Ottawa champions as worthy holders of the Stanley Cup.

"The Silver Seven outplayed and outscored my Nuggets by a wide margin," he conceded. "But remember, my boys came here sadly out of shape after their long journey."

He congratulated Frank McGee on his record-setting performance – 14 goals in the 23-2 second game victory. "And Mr. McGee," he added, turning toward the beaming Ottawa star. "You might have scored twice that number if it hadn't been for young Forrest, my goalie. Never before has a goalie given up so many goals and yet played so magnificently. Many years from now, when hockey people marvel over the 14-goal record, they may suspect that young Forrest must have been a player with little talent. But such is not the case, as every person in this room knows."

Albert, sitting among his teammates, blushed when cries of "Hear, hear!" and a burst of applause filled the room.

Mr. Murphy, an official with the Ottawa Hockey Club, then stood up and complimented the Nuggets on their sportsmanship and fair play. He said they had shown the utmost courage in undertaking an incredible journey from the Yukon to the nation's capital in the dead of winter. He said they had added an amazing chapter to hockey's history book, and that a hundred years hence hockey people would read about their saga and shake their heads in disbelief.

The trustees of the Stanley Cup then presented the gleaming trophy to the Ottawas.

It's astonishing that such a little trophy can create so much excitement among hockey fans, Albert thought.

Then, to his surprise, he heard his name being announced. The trustees of the Stanley Cup had just declared Albert Forrest the most valuable player on the Yukon challengers. Albert shook his head in disbelief. He turned to Norman Watt and said, "Why me? I let in so many goals."

"Because you deserve it, lad," laughed Norman, rising with the others in a standing ovation. Albert rose and limped up to the podium where he was presented with a silver medallion.

Albert knew he was expected to say something. Some of the players shouted, "Speech, speech!" But he felt so out of place, so unprepared. So he began by reading aloud the inscription on the medallion: "To A. Forrest, most valuable player, Dawson City Nuggets, Stanley Cup challengers, 1905."

Then he looked out at the crowd and smiled. He said, "This is the first speech I've ever made so it'll be a short one. Nobody likes to lose or be humiliated and I wish with all my heart I had been able to stop the great players on the Ottawas. I would feel ashamed if I thought I had not done my best but I know in my heart that I did. I have learned a lesson this week, that sometimes a man's best isn't good enough, especially if he's playing the greatest players in the world."

He smiled again, this time toward the tables where the Silver Seven were seated. They all smiled back.

"I know why winning this award makes me feel so good," Albert continued. "It tells me that not everybody thinks of me as a loser. And if the Silver Seven go down in history as one of the greatest teams ever, which I'm sure they will, I can always say that I helped them gain that well-deserved reputation."

Everybody laughed when Albert said that.

"And if the name Forrest should forever be listed in hockey's record book as the youngest goalie or the goalie who gave up the most goals ever in a Stanley Cup game, at least the name Forrest shall be there.

"Gentlemen, playing in the Stanley Cup matches has been the highlight of my life, my biggest thrill by far. And when I get back to Dawson and I wonder if this great adventure really happened or was all just a dream, I'll have this fine medallion to look at, to remind me that I indeed had my chance to play for Lord Stanley's cup, that it really happened to me, and I can assure you I'll never, never forget it.

"God bless you all and thank you very much."

17

A Mystery Revealed

The train conductor's cry of "All aboard" signaled departure time for the Dawson City Nuggets. Having had their Stanley Cup hopes crushed by Frank McGee and the Silver Seven, they would now try to establish some sort of winning record against less formidable opposition. If they could win five or six games in a row, they'd be invited to Pittsburgh for a three-game series before heading back to Dawson.

Caroline had come down to the station to see Albert off. They stood on the platform saying their goodbyes, thinking of the good times they'd enjoyed in the past few days.

Albert hoped his teammates weren't watching them from the train windows. If they were, he knew he'd be in for a ribbing the moment he stepped on board.

He took Caroline's gloved hand in one of his.

"We'll meet again, Caroline," he said. "Somewhere, somehow. I'm sure of it."

"I feel the same way, Albert," she replied. "But I fear your future will be so filled with so many exciting adventures that you may forget me. I've enjoyed our time together so much. I'll take a lot of happy memories with me when I go back to Vancouver tomorrow."

Albert smiled. "I'll never forget you, Caroline. But look! I have something for you, something that I've always treasured and I want you to have. But promise you won't open it now."

He handed her a small box wrapped in tissue.

"On the train tomorrow, on your way back west, you can open it. There's a note inside explaining why my little gift is so meaningful."

She showed him her lovely smile and thanked him. Then she reached into her purse.

"I have a small gift for you, too," she said, squeezing his hand. "We do think alike, don't we? Let's do this. I'll open my gift at noon tomorrow and you open yours then, too. Precisely at noon. That way we'll both be thinking of each other at the very same moment."

She handed him a neatly-wrapped box and a small pink envelope.

Behind them, the train gave a little lurch.

"I'd better go," he said. Still, he clung to her hand, unwilling to release it.

Then he took a quick breath, leaned over and kissed her on the lips. She kissed him back. It was the first time either had kissed or been kissed. It was a very special moment in their young lives, one they would long remember.

Then the train was moving and Albert turned and nimbly jumped on board. He stood on the steps of the pullman, leaning out, waving to Caroline as the train chugged out of the station, gathering speed. Caroline waved a slim arm in return. The train glided into the first turn of the tracks and suddenly she was gone.

The next day, Albert waited impatiently for noon hour to arrive. He was anxious to open the small box Caroline had given him. Both the box and the card sat in his lap.

Finally, after checking his pocket watch a dozen times, the hands stood straight up. It was time to undo the wrapping. He opened the box and looked inside. Then his eyes opened wide and he gasped.

"How in the world . . . how is this possible?" he said half aloud. His forehead was locked in a frown. From the box he took a talisman, his talisman, his good luck charm. But it couldn't be. For his talisman was in the box he'd given Caroline.

Then the answer came to him. It was the only answer. He tore open the envelope and eagerly read Caroline's note.

Dear Albert:
I want you to have this, my most cherished possession. It's a rare talisman, something my father gave to me many years ago when I was just a child. I believe it has brought me comfort and good fortune over the years. My father believes it even helped to save my life one time when I was young. Did I tell you about the time I nearly died under an avalanche once? It was the winter my family started out for the Yukon gold fields. But we didn't get very far. We lost everything one dreadful day at the Chilkoot Pass. Tons of snow came rolling down on us and I was buried alive for a time. Only quick work by a young boy saved my life. He pulled me out, unconscious. I never did learn his name. My father once told me that someday I might want to give my talisman to someone else, but only to someone very special. I suppose I would have given it to the boy who saved my life but I never saw him again. Now I'm glad I saved it for you, for you are someone very special.
I'll always remember you, Albert, and hope we'll meet again.

Love, Caroline.

Albert sat back, astonished. He took a deep breath and stared at the talisman. Caroline was the girl he'd pulled from the deep snow of the Chilkoot Pass on the day of the avalanche. How incredible that they should meet again, and not know it until they exchanged talismans.

It's a huge country we live in, he thought. But it's a small one too, especially when two people involved in a life-and-death experience can meet several years later by chance on a train. Not only meet but become best friends.

He held the talisman aloft.

Perhaps it wasn't all luck that brought us together again, he thought. Perhaps her talisman and mine possess some magical qualities that can't be understood. Perhaps Caroline and I were destined to meet again no matter what.

93

He laughed at the thought of Caroline opening his gift at that very moment, then reading his note, so similar to her own. He imagined her look of astonishment. He pictured her bright eyes shining and her smile of delight when she finally understood the meaning of the second talisman.

18

A Reunion with Evelyne

The hockey team's tour of the Maritimes was a huge success. Weldy Young, bitterly disappointed over missing the championship series in Ottawa, finally caught up with the team. He'd been delayed by snowstorms along the trail from Dawson to Whitehorse and suffered frostbite to both feet. His presence in the lineup strengthened the Nuggets' attack and they won game after game.

Albert received a lot of attention wherever the Nuggets played. Word of his sensational goaltending in the Ottawa games had spread throughout the east. Sportswriters covering the games on the tour wrote glowing reports about him. Many of them found it difficult to believe he'd been scored on twenty-three times in one of the games with Ottawa. Others were surprised to discover he was only seventeen and had taken up goaltending only a short time prior to the big Stanley Cup series.

His reputation as a speedskater had also preceded him. Most of the newspapers carried lengthy stories about his victory over Frank McGee and several times he was asked to skate against the fastest local skaters. He always agreed and never lost a race.

When the Maritime tour was over, Colonel Boyle took Albert aside and said, "I have good news for you, son. I've arranged a special game for the Nuggets in Three Rivers. I know how much it means for you to play there." It also meant a lot to Colonel Boyle for a game to be played there, for, with Albert's growing reputation, the Nuggets' share of the gate receipts would be impressive.

Albert was delighted with the news. He had many happy memories of growing up in the Three Rivers area. He was excited about seeing his old friends and relatives again, especially his sister Evelyne.

Later, Colonel Boyle took Albert aside again and confessed he'd made one little mistake when he booked the Nuggets into Three Rivers, a mistake in the form of a little boast. It was a boast Albert should know about.

"What kind of a boast?" asked Albert, puzzled. "And what does it have to do with me?"

"When they told me the Three Rivers team was an excellent club," Colonel Boyle explained, "with some of the best skaters and scorers in eastern Canada, it just popped out of me, Albert."

"What popped out of you, Colonel Boyle?"

"Well, I told them I didn't care how good their players were because my goalie Albert would keep them off the scoresheet. I told them you would shut them out."

"Colonel Boyle, you boasted that I would play in Three Rivers and not give up a single goal? Do you know how difficult it is to get a shutout? Especially now, near the end of our tour. We're all so tired. I can tell you flat-out, Colonel Boyle, I doubt very much if I'll get a shutout against Three Rivers."

"Now wait a minute, son," Colonel Boyle said, taking Albert by the shoulder. "Don't say that. You see, the men from Three Rivers laughed at me when I said you'd shut them out, so I got angry and, and, and . . .".

"And what, Colonel Boyle?"

"Well, I said if you didn't get a shutout in Three Rivers, they could keep the gate receipts. They could have all the money."

"Keep the gate receipts!" Albert exploded. "But Colonel Boyle, we've been splitting the gate receipts with the other teams we've met so far. The biggest money-maker on our tour could be the game in Three Rivers. And you said we need every penny from the gate receipts to pay our way home."

"I know that, Albert. I know I shouldn't have said what I did to those fellows. I shouldn't have lost my temper. But what's done is done. I can't go back on my word now. So it's all up to you. You've just got to shut them out when we get to Three Rivers."

In Quebec, Albert was pleased when most people spoke to him in French, the language he'd known and loved as a child. In the Yukon, the Forrest family still spoke French, but mostly in their home.

Albert had a full day to spend in Three Rivers. He hurried to his aunt's house where he was thrilled to see his sister Evelyne again. They hugged and kissed and conversed excitedly in both French and English. He told her all about life in Dawson City. She had never been able to fully understand why she had been left behind when the family had moved to the gold fields. When she talked about it, she began to weep.

Albert tried to console her. Then he tried to explain. She had been so young and frail when the gold rush began. The family doctor had advised against travel, especially if she had to cross mountain ranges and sleep in a tent. So, reluctantly, their father had left her behind, promising to send for her soon.

"He thought he'd find lots of gold and you'd be with us in no time," Albert went on. "But it never happened. He's searched everywhere but he's found only enough to get by on. There was never enough extra money to bring you to us."

"It looks to me like Daddy cares more for that silly gold than he does for his only daughter," she sobbed.

Albert was silent. It was difficult to deny that his father, like most of the men who rushed to the Klondike, had put gold-seeking ahead of everything else. Gold had a strange effect on men. He'd seen brother pitted against brother, father against son, in disputes over mining claims. When the gold rush began, he'd heard how men in far-off places had cashed in their savings, left wives and children behind, never to see them again. The mad rush to the gold fields consumed them. Many died there, of sickness, of exposure to sub-zero temperatures, of broken hearts and broken dreams.

Albert could understand Evelyne's feelings. And he found it difficult to defend his father.

"The lust for gold has had a terrible impact on our family, Evelyne," Albert said. "It has pulled us apart from you. No amount of gold is worth that. I know Dad still loves you. He's told me so many times. And Mom misses you terribly. Dad says he's going to strike gold soon. Says he's sure of it. If he does, then we'll be rich and you can come live with us."

"Oh, I'd love that, Albert," she laughed, throwing her arms around his neck. "I'd love to be with my brothers again."

As Albert rushed through the streets of Three Rivers on his way to the arena, he thought of his parents and the decision they'd made so many years ago. How could they leave a sweet little girl like Evelyne behind when they left for the Klondike? What if I'd been the baby in the family? Would I have spent the last few years living with relatives, wondering if I was ever going to see my family again? It's not right, deserting a child to run off and chase a dream of riches in some distant gold field. I'm going to have a serious talk with my dad when I get back to Dawson, Albert thought. I'll soon be eighteen and I have the right to speak my mind about Evelyne. She's been away from us for too long.

That night, with Evelyne and her aunt in attendance, Albert played superbly. In the back of his mind, he kept thinking of the gate receipts and how much money would be lost if he made even one mistake. His eyes followed every turn of the puck and he was prepared for every shot. The Three Rivers team did have excellent forwards, players with speed, tricky moves and heavy shots. But Albert blocked everything they threw at him. He kept the Three Rivers team off the scoresheet and Dawson won 4-0.

When the bell clanged to end the contest, Albert's teammates rushed over and hoisted him onto their shoulders.

"You've saved us, again, Albert," one of them shouted. "We're going to get our money."

"Yes, and we should buy a gag with some of it," Albert

laughed. "It may be the only way to keep Colonel Boyle from making foolish wagers on us."

Evelyne was still clapping her hands together after all the other applause had died away. When Albert met her after the game she hugged him and said, "Oh, Albert. I want to be a hockey player when I get older. Just like my big brother. Can girls play hockey, Albert?"

He laughed and said, "Yes, there are many girls playing hockey, Evelyne. Why shouldn't you be a player if you want to be? If you make up your mind to do something in life, then you should go ahead and do it."

Then he added, "I just wish hockey players were paid to play the game. Then I'd have enough money to take you home with me."

19

To Montreal and Pittsburgh

Before leaving for western Canada, the Nuggets were invited to play a game in hockey-mad Montreal and a series of games in Pittsburgh, Pennsylvania.

After the triumph in Three Rivers, it was only natural that a game should be arranged in Montreal. "After all, the Montreal Wanderers are almost as good as the Ottawa champions," said Colonel Boyle. "And we'll be going through Montreal on our way to Pittsburgh, anyway . . ."

The game in Montreal was a brilliant one and Albert was in peak form against the talented Wanderers. Dawson City squeaked through with a 3-2 win. At half time, Albert amazed the fans when he beat three of the Wanderers' best in a speed skating race around the rink.

"The more we win, the more I love to play," said Sureshot Kennedy, who scored two goals against the Wanderers. "Now let's go to Pittsburgh and see who's ready to face us there."

"But they'll have no ice in Pittsburgh," Albert said to Randy McLennan. "The weather is turning warm, and all their ice will have melted."

Randy laughed. "Of course they'll have ice in Pittsburgh," he said. "Perfect ice. A few years ago they installed artificial ice in the Steel City. They have it in New York, Baltimore and Washington too. It's the coming thing. Someday there'll be artificial ice in every arena in the land. I'll bet on it."

What a marvelous idea, thought Albert. Whoever invented artificial ice deserves a medal. Imagine playing hockey in the spring of the year without having to wade through two inches of water. He had heard of one Stanley Cup game where the water was so deep one player splashed it in the opposing goalie's eyes, temporarily blinding him while a teammate scored with the puck. Albert couldn't wait to skate on the artificial ice in Pittsburgh.

The Nuggets won all three of the games they played in Pittsburgh and Albert received several standing ovations for his spectacular play. When a reporter asked him why he skated around with his head down during breaks in the play, he answered, "I'm trying to see the pipes under the ice. You know, the ones that carry the brine that makes the water freeze. Randy told me there are several miles of pipe running lengthwise under the ice. But they're really hard to see."

In the final Pittsburgh game, Albert astonished the fans with a play they would talk about for years afterward. Veteran reporters covering the game said they'd never seen anything like it and never expected to see such a play again.

What prompted the young goalie to do what he did nobody knew, not even Albert himself.

"I just reacted," he told reporters who clustered around him when the game was over. He winked at them and said, "But aren't you pleased I gave you something to write about?"

What Albert did was score a goal.

Nobody had ever seen a goalie score a goal, not the fans, the referee, or any of the players on the ice. Nobody. Not even Randy McLennan or Weldy Young, both of whom had been playing hockey practically since the game was invented.

Late in the final game, with the score tied 3-3, the Nuggets began to tire. One of them tried to lift the puck down the ice but he fanned on the shot and the puck rolled dangerously close to Albert's goal. When players from both teams converged on it, they collided and suddenly the ice was littered with falling bodies.

Somehow, from under the pile of players, the puck squirted free. And it came right to Albert.

Instinctively, Albert cradled the puck on his stick and dashed up the ice with it. The legs that helped forge his reputation as a champion speedskater propelled him over the hard artificial ice with amazing speed.

Two of the Pittsburgh players not trapped in the pileup scrambled back to protect their goalie. Then they spun around to face the onrushing Albert.

The fans, meanwhile, were on their feet, screaming encouragement to Albert.

"Go, lad, go!"

One of the Pittsburgh defenders lunged at Albert. But the goaltender slipped the puck through the man's legs and darted around him. He pulled the same trick on the second defender, leaving the man spinning in his wake.

Albert sped in on goal and with a flick of his wrists sent the puck spinning into the upper corner of the cage. The goal judge waved his hankie wildly and then ran over to Albert and pumped his hand.

The Pittsburgh goalie hauled himself up and fished the puck out of the net. A good sport, he grinned at Albert. Then, with his stick, he flipped the disc toward Albert, who caught it and waved it high in the air. The fans roared their appreciation. Albert, not knowing quite what to do next, made several small bows to all corners of the arena.

Not only was Albert's goal the game winner but his feat was described in all the papers the next day. Sports fans read about it from New York to California. The Americans loved Albert and urged him to stay on in Pittsburgh. They wanted him to join their hockey team the following winter and promised him a good job in the steel mills.

Albert was tempted. Not only was the money good but he enjoyed the reception he'd received from the friendly Americans. But the smoky Pittsburgh skies, fouled by the emissions from the mills, made him yearn for his northern home, where fresh mountain breezes brought scents from afar, and where fresh spring water, sipped from two cupped hands, could quench a thirst like no water to be found in Pennsylvania. Or anywhere else, Albert decided.

The Nuggets were on the move again, first north, back into Canada at Niagara Falls. What a wonder the great falls are, thought Albert, oblivious to the spray from the cataract that drenched him as he stared in awe at the tons of water plunging into the gorge below. Far below, a small boat bravely danced in the turbulence, as if daring the mighty torrent to submerge her. Then Albert heard his teammates calling. The train that would take them to Toronto had arrived. Another would take them west. Their long tour would soon be over.

20

The Journey Home

The Nuggets played their final game in Brandon, Manitoba where they walloped a tough local team 9-1 on a surface that was soft as a pillow. The rest of the tour was canceled. It was the end of a remarkable season.

Spring was in the air, temperatures soared and ice turned to water. Roads everywhere were soupy with mud.

In Brandon, ladies crossed the broad avenues at their peril, lifting their long, heavy skirts ankle high as they tip-toed over narrow boards to the safety of the wooden sidewalks on the far side. If a board tipped or a high button shoe slipped, the lady stumbled into the mud, emitting a shriek of despair. If she was single and attractive, a local lad would leap up from the bench in front of the billiard hall, plunge into the street and scoop her to safety. It was said that Brandon's muddy streets precipitated many a courtship and marriage.

The Nuggets gathered at Brandon's finest dining hall for a final meeting of the team. Several players had already stated they would not be going back to Dawson. Others wanted to delay a return while they visited friends and relatives in various parts of Canada.

Of the players that began the great Stanley Cup journey, only Albert was anxious to get back to the Yukon. He longed for his log home and his loving family. He yearned for the vast stretches of wilderness that made the Yukon such a spectacular place.

He thought of his friend Robert Service, the English poet who encouraged Albert to experience the joys of reading. It was Service who had loaned him several wonderful books which enriched his world. And it was Service who shared Albert's love for the Yukon's craggy peaks and sparkling rivers.

He could understand how a man like Service came to the Yukon, not to chase gold, but to scribble poems describing the sheer beauty of the place.

> It's a great, big broad land
> Way up yonder,
> It's the forests where silence
> has lease;
> It's the beauty that thrills me
> with wonder.
> It's the stillness that fills me
> with peace.

Perhaps it was the influence of his friend Service that prompted Albert to write a couple of poems of his own. One was to Caroline. On the train to Pittsburgh, on Valentine's Day, he had written in his diary:

> Oh, Caroline, sweet Caroline,
> Say you will, will, will be mine,
> I'll treat you swell, I'll treat you fine,
> I'll be your lifelong Valentine.

He'd even written a poem about his role in the Stanley Cup series but he didn't think it was much good.

> Yes, I'm the boy who stood in goal
> Facing rubber hurled at me,
> Yes, I'm the lad whose job it was
> To stop the Great McGee.
> I tried my best but failed the test
> For the record shows that he,
> Scored fourteen goals in a single game,
> And all of them on me.
> They cheered him loud, they cheered him long,

It was quite a sight to see,
Each time he scored, the more they roared,
"You're our hero, Frank McGee."
It's true I was the victim of
His record-setting spree,
What's more, his mates began to score
'Til they totaled twenty-three.
Oh, someday when I'm old and gray,
With my grandson on my knee,
I'll tell him of the night I faced
The mighty Frank McGee.
I'll talk about his blazing shot,
And his boundless energy,
And how he played with one bad eye,
Why, the man could barely see.
I'll talk about the Stanley Cup,
How it slipped away from me,
And all because of hockey's best,
Old one-eyed Frank McGee.

It was an emotional parting. The players had traveled thousands of miles together, sharing an adventure unlike any other in the history of sport. It was true they had failed in their bid to win the Stanley Cup. But they had played some spectacular hockey in all of their other games. Once they found their hockey legs, and with Weldy Young punching in goal after goal, they were almost unbeatable.

There were embraces and firm handshakes when they parted. And words of "God bless" and "Good luck" and "See you again, mate." There was the realization that they might never be together again, certainly not as hockey players, not as a close-knit team in search of an elusive cup. That's when faces turned away and calloused hands brushed brimming eyes.

Certainly Albert's eyes were moist. For he realized he loved these men. Some more than others. But even the undisciplined ones, the few who put their own selfish interest ahead of the team, had qualities he respected. Nobody could make Albert laugh harder than Sureshot Kennedy. Nobody was more generous with his money – even if it was won in an all-night poker game – than Gloomy Johnstone.

Now, with their time together as teammates running out, Gloomy approached him and apologized for his conduct on the train to Ottawa.

"You were right to get mad at me on the train that night," he told Albert. "At first I wanted to wring your neck when you gave me what-for in front of my friends. Then, when I thought about it, I realized they weren't the kind of friends I wanted. Not like my friends on the team. You shook me up that night and I hope you noticed I behaved myself a lot better after that."

Albert said he had noticed. He said he was proud of Gloomy's behavior on and off the ice. They shook hands. Albert grinned at Gloomy, whose face lit up for the first time in weeks.

Albert was happy to hear Randy McLennan state he would be returning to Dawson in a week or two. Throughout the trip, nobody had been nicer to Albert or given him better advice than the good doctor. Someday soon, back in Dawson, he would ask Randy for a lot more advice. Albert wanted to know what qualities it took to become a man of medicine.

He knew all of these men so well. He knew their strengths and weaknesses and thought he understood them all. They had been the best men, and the best hockey players, next to the Ottawas, he had ever seen. It's true they had doubted him at first. They had questioned his ability, thought him too green. But he had proven himself and had quickly become one of them. They all respected him. He felt certain of it. And it made him feel good.

He thought of the words his father had said when he left Dawson weeks earlier. "You'll have learned a lot more about your teammates and their character before this trip is over."

Hockey would never be the same in Dawson without these men. Albert would play for the Nuggets again – perhaps play for many years – but never again with players so talented. The gold rush, which lured the hockey men to the Klondike in the first place, was over. More people were rushing to get out of Dawson than were rushing in. And Dawson City's chances of winning the Stanley Cup were over too.

There'll be no more challenges from the Yukon, thought Albert. Not for years and years. Perhaps not in my lifetime. The thought of it made him sad – as sad as the thought of his father, forever seeking the elusive metal, so intent on finding it he'd lost a daughter, stubbornly insisting there were fortunes to be found in places others had abandoned.

On the train to Vancouver that night he wrote in his diary:

Hockey was meant to be fun, and it is. I'll always enjoy it. But on this trip I have taken the game very seriously. Given it all my energy. Now it may be time to look in other directions.

A voice inside me is saying, "Albert, open up your eyes to all the other adventures in life that are there for the exploring. In the weeks ahead, think of what you want to do with the rest of your life. And don't be afraid to aim high. There may be a place for you in politics or government. Perhaps you have the potential to become a doctor like Randy, or a writer like Robert Service.

Before I left on this trip, I would never have dared to dream of such things. I was so unsure of myself, so lacking in confidence. But then, I never thought I could become a goalie, either. And now, despite old Frank McGee, I think I'm a pretty good goalie. I feel that I can accomplish many things in life if I set my mind to it. And it excites me.

I wish I could see Caroline when we reach Vancouver but I know there won't be time. I'll have to run from the station to the dock if I hope to board the steamer to Skagway. I wonder if Caroline and I will ever be together. Time will tell. When I think of her I feel light-headed. Her sweet name is always on my mind. And when I looked into the black glass of the train window a moment ago, her lovely face smiled back at me. And I heard the words she whispered when we parted. "I hope we'll meet again, Albert. I think you're wonderful."

21

The Soapy Smith Saga

It was a lonely trip west without his mates and with such deep thoughts on his mind.

The voyage from Vancouver to Skagway was miserable. Heavy rain and stiff winds whipped the waves and kept Albert in his bunk, once again a victim of the seasickness he so dreaded.

In Skagway, he walked the pleasant streets, killing time before catching the train to Whitehorse. He smiled when he passed the beach and thought of how close he came to being kidnaped by the captain of the *Nellie Glenn.*

On a side street, Albert noticed a small building with a sign above the door: Soapy Smith's Saloon. Soapy Smith? He remembered Soapy Smith, the gentleman who had given Albert and his bothers some sweets and apples years earlier. The same man who took pity on Brandy's owner and gave him money for a ticket home.

Albert tried the door to the saloon. It was locked. He peered through a window and saw chairs turned upside down on the tops of tables. There was a long polished mahogany bar and a piano in the corner. This place hasn't been open for business in a long time, Albert thought.

Albert decided to get a haircut. He asked the barber if he knew the name Soapy Smith. The man laughed and said, "Course I do, son. That's one name everybody knows."

"Can you tell me where he is?" Albert asked.

"I sure can and he's likely to be there for quite awhile," the barber replied. He nodded toward a side window and for a second Albert thought the man meant Soapy was just outside. "He's resting quietly about a mile from here, up yonder in the graveyard."

"Soapy's dead?"

The barber chuckled. "If he isn't then the folks in town made a horrible mistake a few years ago when they buried him." He chuckled again and looked through his scissors to see if Albert appreciated his little joke.

"Mr. Smith was very kind to my brothers and me years ago," Albert said. "I'm surprised he's dead."

The barber put down his scissors. "Son, let me tell you the true story of Soapy Smith and how he wound up in the graveyard with a bullet hole in his chest big enough to drive a team of huskies through.

"For a long time, Soapy Smith was the most powerful man in Skagway. Later, we found out he was also the most crooked. Old Soapy was a smooth operator, he was that, a man with real southern charm. But while Soapy was busy charming us all, he was also busy recruiting a gang of misfits and cutthroats. Scruffiest bunch you ever did see. Mean customers, all of them. And he hired some con men, too. Smooth talkers like himself who knew all the tricks. They'd fleece the newcomers, the goldseekers, out of all they owned one way or another. They'd doctor a man's drink in Soapy's saloon and he'd wake up in some dark alley with his pockets empty. Or they'd win his cash in crooked card games.

"Soapy and his cronies – one of them even posed as a kind-hearted minister – would meet the new arrivals and befriend them. Soapy would offer to store their belongings in his shed free of charge. If they accepted his offer, he'd go through their possessions and get a sense of whether they were rich or poor. If they had wealth, Soapy and his boys would soon separate them from it.

"For a long time, nobody connected Soapy with the crimes for he always played the role of a model citizen. Even his victims looked on him as a generous man. After being assaulted and robbed, they'd show up bruised and bloody and with empty pokes. Soapy would cluck his tongue, feigning sympathy. He'd even reach in his pocket and give his victims cash for a ticket back to wherever they came from. Soapy was smart. Getting rid of them by putting them on the next boat meant they'd never come back to testify against him if his role was ever discovered."

Albert was astonished. That's exactly what happened to Brandy's owner. And now I know why Soapy was so kind to us, thought Albert. He was sizing us up. We're lucky we weren't beaten up and robbed. Soapy may have been smart but Dad was smarter. He saw right through Soapy.

"How did they finally catch on to him?" Albert asked.

"One day a fellow named Stewart came back from the gold fields. He was headed home to Seattle to see his wife and kiddies after months of back-breaking work in the mines. Had a poke of $2800 in his pocket. Soapy's men stole it from him. So Stewart went straight to Frank Reid, who had just been named to head up a citizen's committee formed to clean up Skagway. For weeks, Reid had been urging the citizens to stop Soapy's shenanigans but nobody listened. Everybody was terrified of Soapy and his boys. We'd jump right off the boardwalk into the mud when his toughs came strolling down the street.

"But Frank Reid, bless him, wasn't afraid. He went to Soapy's saloon and ordered him to give Stewart back his gold. Soapy just laughed at him. Said Stewart must have lost his gold in a poker game. Then Soapy got mad and ordered Reid from his saloon, ran him off at gunpoint.

"That did it. Reid went home and loaded his rifle. Sent word to Soapy to meet him down on the dock. Soapy grabbed his rifle and his six guns and told his pals, 'I'll go down there and teach Frank Reid a lesson or two.'

"He swaggered down the main street, a large crowd following him. Soapy grinned and waved to them. I was there, right in the middle of the pack. We all thought it was going to be curtains for Frank Reid.

"At the dock, the two men faced each other. I thought Reid looked very brave. He didn't flinch when Soapy gave him quite a tongue-lashing. I remember Reid replied in a strong voice, 'Say what you want, Soapy Smith, but today marks a turning point. Your days are numbered. You'll steal no more. I'm telling you to leave town and take your gang of thieves with you.'

"Soapy's face turned bright crimson. 'I should have had you killed a long time ago, Reid,' he shouted for all to hear. He waved his rifle toward Reid, perhaps just to scare him. But Reid saw it as a threat to his life. He snatched up his own rifle and took aim at Soapy. Suddenly, it was Soapy who showed fear. 'Don't shoot, Frank! For God's sake, don't shoot!' But Reid's finger was already squeezing the trigger."

Albert, listening intently, let out a long breath. "So that's how Soapy Smith was killed," he said quietly.

"Wait!" replied the barber. "There's more to the story. You see, there was a little twist of fate. We'll call it that anyway. When Frank Reid pulled the trigger, his gun failed to fire. It happens sometimes. So all we heard was a loud click. Reid stood there with a puzzled look on his face.

"Soapy, who'd been terrified of dying a second earlier, started to laugh. Now he had the upper hand. He raised his rifle, and gleefully pumped a slug into the astonished Reid. Caught him right in the stomach and Reid went down, blood gushing from a huge wound.

"Soapy must have felt he had the right to shoot Reid. After all, Reid had fired first. Or tried to. Everybody'd seen it. Any jury would call Soapy's actions self-defense. Especially a Skagway jury. And all of Soapy's men would back him up.

"But Soapy made a big mistake. He didn't finish the job. He turned to acknowledge the cheers of his gang members. And that cost him his life. Frank Reid, barely conscious, mustered enough strength to raise his rifle and take a second shot at Soapy. And this time he put a hole right through old Soapy's chest. I'll tell you, boy, that stopped the laughter. Soapy Smith was dead before he hit the ground."

"Tell me, mister, what happened to Frank Reid? Did he recover from his wound?" Albert asked the barber.

"No, son, I'm afraid he didn't. But he died a hero. Had the biggest funeral in Skagway's history. He's buried up there in the graveyard, so close to old Soapy they could almost hold hands. As if they'd want to. Poor Frank. If his rifle hadn't misfired that day, he'd be mayor of this town.

"And you should see the monument we erected over his grave. On its face is a simple inscription. 'He gave his life for the honor of Skagway'. Smith has a wooden marker over his resting place. It's all chipped in places where souvenir hunters have been helping themselves to pieces of it."

Albert had hung on every word. He'd never heard such a fascinating story before. It was like something out of the wild west.

I guess it proves, he thought, how easily we can be deceived by men who pretend they are something they're not. Again, he felt a warm regard for his father. Dad was suspicious of Soapy. He saw something in him I failed to see.

22

Dawson at Last

Albert was on the train to Whitehorse. The weather cleared and he felt the excitement that comes on the last leg of a long journey. With March about to give way to April, Albert calculated he'd covered close to 14,000 miles since he left Dawson the previous December.

He had money in his pocket. Colonel Boyle had divided the profits from the exhibition games with the Nuggets. It wasn't a large amount but more than enough for Albert. He hadn't expected to come back with anything.

In Whitehorse he bought a bicycle, a used one. And a derby hat, a new one. And a little brooch for Caroline, a pretty one. The hat made him look older, more dashing. Why, I guess I am a man now, Albert thought, peering into the mirror. He tipped his derby this way and that. Well, almost a man. At least I'm not the shy, awkward, innocent young fellow I was when I began this trip.

The bicycle didn't take him far. The spring thaw transformed the trail to Dawson into a river of mud. In other places, the trail refused to heed the nudge of spring. Hard-packed snow and chunks of ice made bicycle travel impossible. So Albert left his wheels at one of the North West Mounted Police outposts and began to walk the rest of the way.

Within a week, he was home. What emotions tugged at his heart as he walked that last mile into Dawson. His pace quickened and a smile broke across his sun-bronzed face the moment he saw the familiar buildings.

On the edge of town, he stopped to dust off his new derby. He placed it on his head at a jaunty angle, adjusted his heavy backpack for the last time, and walked briskly into town.

As he strode down Front Street, the first man to see him shouted, "Hey, it's Albert. Young Albert's finally home from the playoffs."

Others took up the cry. In seconds Albert was surrounded. Excited citizens crowded around, pounding his back, asking questions. They were so happy to see him.

How his family got there so quickly Albert didn't know. But there they were, running down the street toward him, calling his name, waving their arms.

Brandy reached him first, barking a welcome. The husky bounded into his arms, forcing him to stagger back. Brandy licked his face, his ears and nibbled at his hand.

And then he was caught in the warm embrace of his family. He was smothered with hugs and kisses. His mother squeezed him so hard his hat flew off his head but his father reached out and caught it before it hit the ground.

When Paul was able to get a word in, he looked up at the bronzed face of his brother and said, "Did you bring me some apples, Albert?"

Albert smiled and reached into his pack. He produced a small bag of apples.

"There you go, Paul. I brought them all the way from Vancouver."

Albert turned to Emil. "And here's the puck you wanted. It's one of about a hundred Frank McGee shot into my goal in Ottawa. I even had him autograph it for you."

Albert had gifts for his parents, too. Lace handkerchiefs for his mother and a photograph of the Parliament Buildings in Ottawa for his father.

"See right here, Dad," Albert said. "It's signed by the Governor General. And that's his real signature. I know because I met him. He signed it for me. And he invited me back to Ottawa next year to defend the skating title I won. I probably won't go because it'll be too expensive but it's nice to be invited, isn't it?"

"It's wonderful, son," Mr. Forrest said. "Wonderful. Hey, everybody, let's celebrate Albert's return."

"Yes, let's all go into the Frontier Hotel and have some cake and lemonade," Mrs. Forrest said. "Then Albert can tell us all about his adventures." She took her son's arm. "Are you hungry, Albert? And did you enjoy your trip?"

"Yes, I'm famished, Mom," Albert said with a laugh. "And I had a marvelous time. I saw Evelyne in Three Rivers and she really misses us all. Later, I want to talk to you and Dad about Evelyne. Oh, and I met the best-looking girl on the train. I'll tell you all about her when we get home. And I bought this wonderful hat in Whitehorse. Don't you just love it?" He placed it on his mother's head.

The Forrests mounted the steps leading up to the hotel. The crowd followed at a respectful distance. Albert couldn't have drawn more attention if he'd been a prospector who'd just hit paydirt.

When Albert reached the top step, somebody below shouted. "We're real proud of you, Albert. We want you to know that. You didn't win the Cup but you helped to put Dawson on the map. We heard you did a wonderful job in goal despite the score. So welcome home."

Albert turned and grinned. "Thank you," he said. "I wish I could have brought back the Stanley Cup but all I have to show you is this small gold medal." He held the medal aloft. "The Governor General gave it to me."

Paul piped up proudly. "It was for winning the big skating race in Ottawa. Albert beat Frank McGee. Beat him bad, too. Now Albert's the fastest man on ice, anywhere."

The crowd laughed and applauded.

An old miner spoke through his beard. "Was it worth it, Albert? Going all that way in vain. Was it worth it?"

Albert thought for a moment before he replied. He recalled the agony of the long walk to Whitehorse, the fierce winds that tore at his body and the deep snow that numbed his blistered feet. He thought of his narrow escape from the whaling ship. He recalled the majestic peaks of the Rockies, the vast prairie lands, the endless tall forests in Eastern Canada and the charming fishing villages in the Maritimes. Once again he heard Members of Parliament in hot debate. He heard the cheering that followed his stunning victory over the great McGee in the skating race at Government House. He felt a pang, the pain of losing to the Ottawas . . . and by such a large score . . . followed by a feeling of pride, pride at being named his team's most valuable player. He thought of his emotional reunion with Evelyne. He thought of all he'd seen and done, all the lessons he'd learned, all the ways the long journey had shaped and changed him. Finally, he thought of Caroline. He could see her priceless smile, her perfect face.

His fingers closed around the talisman in his pocket and when he spoke his voice was clear and steady.

"Yes, the trip was worth it. If I live a hundred years I don't expect I'll ever have another adventure like this one. Oh, yes, it was worth it. It was surely worth it."

The Rest of the Story

Curious readers may want to know what happened next. In short, what's the rest of the story? What became of Albert Forrest after he returned to Dawson? Did he become a doctor or a writer? Did he ever play big time hockey again or return to Government House for another skating race? Did he marry Caroline? Did his father strike it rich and send for Evelyne as he'd promised he would?

While Albert fulfilled his hockey dream of playing for the Stanley Cup, he was never able to realize some of his other ambitions. He could not afford to attend college so Albert never studied medicine. Nor did he become a full time writer even though several articles he wrote about his trip to Ottawa were printed in the local newspaper, the Klondike Nugget.

Eventually, Albert joined the printing department on the Nugget. *He was a good worker, fast and accurate, the best around, according to his employers. Later, he was offered a position in Juneau, Alaska where he worked in the printing business for many years.*

Albert always retained his love for sport. He won many cycling and speedskating races in the Yukon and Alaska. He played baseball and hockey for many years and turned down several offers to play goal for teams in far off places.

He never returned to Government House to defend his title as the world's fastest skater. Nor did he compete again for the Stanley Cup, although he often longed for another chance to win Lord Stanley's trophy.

Albert's role as a Stanley Cup participant warrants a single line in one of hockey's history books. "He was the youngest goalie who traveled the longest distance (under the most trying conditions) only to lose by the largest margin in playoff history."

Albert and Caroline exchanged letters and cards for many years for each of them continued to have strong feelings for the other. Whenever Albert was depressed and needed a lift, he would take out his talisman and think of Caroline. That always boosted his spirits. But they never married.

Caroline grew up, became a nurse and eventually married a fine young doctor in Vancouver.

Albert, before he left to live in Alaska, fell in love with a dark-eyed Dawson girl. Her name was Parmelia Joyal and they were married in 1910. Albert and Parmelia had four children, three boys and a girl.

Late in his life, after the death of his wife, Albert moved to Everett, Washington, where he lived out his final years in the home of his son Leonard. Albert died on July 28, 1955.

His sister Evelyne waited in vain for that longed-for ticket to join her family in Dawson City. Her hopes of ever seeing them again gradually faded and died. In time, she married kind, gentle Oscar Fontaine of Three Rivers, who showered her with the kind of affection she longed for from the family she never knew. Evelyne grew up to be an excellent hockey player and was the star of several women's teams in Quebec. How proud Albert would have been if he could have seen her play! But it was never to be.

Albert's brothers Paul and Emil shared his love for the far north and stayed in the Yukon. As a teenager, Emil suffered a hip injury in a hockey game and walked with a limp for the rest of his life. Paul married and raised a family but Emil remained a life-long bachelor.

Albert's father, frustrated and depressed over his failure to find gold in large amounts, deserted his wife and family one day. His sons searched far and wide for him but were never able to find him. He may have returned to California.

Mrs. Forrest resigned herself to the fact her husband would never be coming back. Over the next few years, she worked at various jobs in

Dawson City and was able to support herself. She was proud of her loving sons, one of whom (Emil) lived at home and took good care of her until her death.

Brandy lived to a ripe old age and sired dozens of Brandy look-alikes. His offspring were renowned for their strength and endurance.

Robert Service became a renowned poet, the "poet of the Yukon" and Colonel Joe Boyle became a famous figure in Canadian and world history. He played an important military role in the first World War. Somehow, he even became a favorite of Marie, Queen of Rumania. She relied on him for advice and guidance. People have written books about Colonel Boyle, the wealthy mining magnate who financed the Nuggets' trip to Ottawa.

In Skagway, thousands of people annually visit the grave sites of Soapy Smith and heroic Frank Reid. There's a particular fascination for the grave of Smith, which had to be fenced off years ago to keep souvenir seekers at arm's length.

Several of the players on the Ottawa Silver Seven performed brilliantly for many years, especially one-eyed Frank McGee. McGee was a chunky, blond handsome man, a team leader with outstanding skills and a winning personality. McGee still holds the single game record for playoff scoring – the 14 goals he scored against Albert on the night of January 16, 1905.

Despite his visual handicap, McGee joined the Canadian army. He was killed in action in the first World War. He and several other members of the Ottawa Silver Seven have been inducted into the Hockey Hall of Fame.

It is not likely Albert's brief career in hockey will ever qualify him for a berth in the Hockey Hall of Fame. But his story deserves to be there. Perhaps, through this book, his remarkable saga will find a niche within those hallowed halls.

While the story of The Youngest Goalie *is based on truth, some of the episodes depicted by the author are purely fictional.*